Salah el Moncef was born in Kuwait City, Kuwait. He is the author of *The Offering*, *Atopian Limits*, and *Art as Pharmakon*. His short fiction, largely focused on the Arab diaspora experience, has been published in numerous British and American magazines and anthologies. He is a five-time Fulbright scholar and a recipient of the Presidential Award for Excellence in the Humanities. El Moncef is Reader in English and Creative Writing at Nantes University, France.

Salah el Moncef

Now and Then

Two Stories

&

Two Essays

PENELOPE BOOKS
PARIS . OXFORD . LOS ANGELES

Penelope Books
2, bis. Rue Dupont de L'Eure
75020 Paris, France

36A Norham Road
Oxford ox2 6SQ, United Kingdom

8605 Santa Monica Blvd
West Hollywood, California, 90069-4109
United States

Copyright © 2023 by Salah el Moncef
All rights reserved under International and Pan-American Conventions.
Printed in the United States of America
First edition, 2023

All characters, localities, and business establishments represented in this book are fictional, and any resemblance to actual places or persons living or dead is purely coincidental.
Publisher's Cataloging-in-Publication data

Library of Congress Cataloging-in-Publication Data
Moncef, Salah el, author.
    Now and Then / by Salah el Moncef.

ISBN: 9782494412002

Cover credits: Pascale Gueret (iStock) / AMR Image (iStock) / anammark (Abobe Stock)

The past is never dead. It's not even past.
William Faulkner, *Requiem for a Nun*

Contents

INTRODUCTION ix

PREFACE TO BENGHAZI xxxv

Benghazi 47

The Night Visitor 113

"A Bridge Too Near" 143

"The Voice of Exile" 155

Introduction

Assuming mankind survives its current battles with unrelenting viral opponents, the "new normal" for the most fortunate among us might include a return to more adventurous travel, pleasurable odysseys that often begin at the airport. And for many flyers, excluding those fantasists who like to impersonate doctors or laboratory scientists, the relegation of surgical masks to desk drawers cluttered with orphaned keys and crumpled receipts will certainly enhance the experience. Longer journeys, however, demand more diversion than unimpeded respiration can supply, immersion in an intriguing memoir or history, for example. In her Introduction to *The Offering* (2015), Mari Ruti recalls such an experience reading Salah el Moncef's "gripping detective story of murder, mayhem, and mental illness" while making the over five-hour flight from Los Angeles to Boston. Captivated by the intricacies of the plot, she was grateful to hear the plane's captain announce that a storm necessitated an hour-long holding pattern before landing, as the delay afforded her more time with this extraordinary novel. As Ruti is quick to explain, however, while readers of *The Offering* are rendered "breathless" by its narrative, this excitement is only one of its attractions; the ambiguity and complexity of the novel's protagonist Tariq Abbassi, for instance, are similarly engaging. The victim of a traumatic brain injury that has shattered his memory of a tragic accident, Tariq hopes to salve the "unspeakable" pain of the event, pain that complicates his attempts to forge a life in Paris and, later, Bordeaux that also *feels* "livable." More broadly, as I underscored in the *Los Angeles Review of*

Books (April 4, 2015), although the narrative of *The Offering* enthralls readers with the mysteries and heart-rending particulars of Tariq's life (and death, as noted in the second paragraph of the Foreword), his struggles are also emblematic of the plight of diasporic subjects who seem never fully at home in their new country—or their old one. The final essay of *Now and Then*, "The Voice of Exile," returns to Tariq, a "displaced Tunisian national and trauma victim" living in France, and so will I in my conclusion.

Like Ruti's Introduction, the back cover of *The Offering* is, for my purposes, also useful because of the quartet of "blurbs" to be found there. Taken together, these endorsements provide a summation of two of the novelist's signal achievements: the "aesthetic elegance" of his prose and his ability to pull off an amazing narrative "trick" in this "postmodern-cum-magical realist" work. Further suggestive of the range of this artistry *and* erudition are the backgrounds of the "blurbists" (a seldom-used designation, thank God!): an accomplished writer and student of language (Rebecca Gowers), and three exceptional poets (Willis Barnstone, Khaled Mattawa, and Philip Metres) whose corpus of work extends to translation, textual criticism, and cultural theory. Albeit helpful in reading *The Offering*, such expertise is perhaps even more welcome in sifting through the nuances of *Now and Then*, a volume of both fiction and speculative criticism. That el Moncef would undertake such a combinatory project is hardly surprising. After all, he is a sophisticated scholar-critic himself and has been for more than two decades as demonstrated by such texts as *Atopian Limits: Questions of Self, Complexity, and Contingency in the Postmodern American Narrative* (2002) and his fine essay "Minor Literature" in *The Oxford Encyclopedia of Literary Theory* (online, 2020; print, 2022). So, while the novella ("Benghazi") and novelette ("The Night Visitor") featured in *Now and Then* are presciently anticipated by these four readers, the volume's two essays epitomizing el Moncef's larger political project demand a slightly different approach.

My purpose here is, first, to sketch preliminary maps of "Benghazi" and "The Night Visitor," then construct routes between the novella and novelette while, on occasion (now and then), slipping away down a few side streets and dark alleys. The major thoroughfares between the pair are both narrative and stylistic; the lesser-traveled roads lead to emotionally resonant moments in each story that dominate characters' memories and instantiate alternatively paralytic and compulsive symptoms. Then, I hope to summarize the arguments of the essays in *Now and Then*, "A Bridge Too Near: Détournement and the Promise of a Transnational Conscience" and "The Voice of Exile," both of which emerge from the discourses of cultural theory, particularly postcolonialism and critiques of nationalism, and both of which posit an alternative to what Benedict Anderson famously termed the "imagined community" of nationhood. My task also includes the forging of connections between el Moncef the theorist and el Moncef the novelist though, like all writers, he is under no obligation to facilitate such pathways. At the dawn of the previous century (and slightly before), Bernard Shaw prefaced his plays and novels with polemics about tenement housing, industrial capitalism, the affective consequences of poverty, and other topics that greatly transcended the scope of the work it preceded; as a novelist, Virginia Woolf refined modernist aesthetics while, as a feminist, she served as a powerful advocate for social equality and the expansion of educational opportunities for women. Yet, because the political aspirations of the essays in *Now and Then* respond directly to the multicultural worlds depicted in el Moncef's fiction, they *should* be read as not only articulating a progressive critique of nationalism, but also as identifying one origin of his characters' internal conflicts.

Although the provenances of the protagonists' conflicts in "Benghazi" and "The Night Visitor" are less convoluted than those plaguing Tariq Abbassi, they are just as crucial to understanding both stories. And their exposition is more straightforward—how could it be otherwise? *The Offering*, as its Foreword clarifies, conveys a story and, at the same time, is "the story of that story": the text's recovery from the "recesses of a near-defunct laptop" owned by its deceased author, its serial rejection by disinterested publishers, its delivery to an American editor who "patched it up as best she could," its typesetting in England, and eventual printing. By contrast, both stories in *Now and Then* begin in a comfortably familiar way: over cups of coffee and conversation. In the opening scene of "Benghazi," Mariam Khaldoon and her husband Basil, a professor at Indiana University in Bloomington, enjoy a sachertorte and coffee on a bright April morning in 1976. He leaves her momentarily, returning with a bulbous envelope with the words "A GET WELL WISH" inscribed in gold letters on the outside. She discovers a gift and note inside, the opening sentences of which suggest both the appropriateness of Basil's gift—an elegant Parker fountain pen—and the existence of a specter from her past impeding her progress as a writer:

> *One way to deal with the sickness of the past would be to assume that some things that made us sick are now essential to our healing in the long run. Please finish your amazing story, and I will proudly translate the rest with as much delight as I translated Part One.*

His alternatively encouraging and pleading tone and the "GET WELL" inscription on the envelope intimate that Mariam's paralysis as a writer is both debilitating and ongoing. *Will* completing her draft function therapeutically in confronting the sickness of her past? The story's introduction ends with her resolve to do just that: "*This is probably the best time to do it—finish what I started."* The best time to confront that "other spring, and "the roiling years that led up to it."

Mariam's project transports readers from 1970s America to Libya in 1942, then earlier to 1939 when her father suffered a fatal heart attack, and finally 1937, the year Benito Mussolini came to Benghazi. Mussolini's visit was a major event for the city, and its planners worked on the pageantry of his arrival as if they were designing an operatic or theatrical production. A platform was erected in the city's central piazza with flags and banners (including the Italian *tricolore*) flanking it on all sides. As Anna Burns notes in her Man Booker Award-winning novel *Milkman* (2018), flags, particularly national flags, were "invented" to be "instinctive and emotional—often pathologically, narcissistically emotional"—and such is the case on this afternoon in Benghazi. When Il Duce, attired in military regalia and astride a black Arabian stallion, entered the square, he was greeted by a "hurricane of cheers and applause"; the crowd's "mad" excitement swelled further when he unsheathed the "Sword of Islam" and waved it triumphantly over his head. The day had been made even more momentous for the Khaldoons when it was announced earlier that not only would Mussolini visit the Scuola Elementare e Media Giovanni Gentile where Mariam, then ten years old, and her older sister Zaynab were students, but that both sisters were chosen to meet him. Zaynab was given the further honor of delivering the school's official welcome. And she did so brilliantly. The sound of her "crystal-clear voice" and flawless Italian when reading the speech caused Mariam to "glow with pride." Even the visiting colonizer was impressed:

> *That achievement had apparently worked its way swiftly into the heart of the semi-clownish tyrant who looked so stiff and flushed, as if straitjacketed in his otherworldly uniform. He raised his eyebrows, popped his eyes wide, and gave my sister a deep nod of respectful admiration.*

Mussolini's nod of approval was accompanied by his enthusiastic "*Brava, brava.*" Yet, with a precocity that seems both telling and discordant, Mariam, who moments earlier had detected in his facial expression the combination of a "crybaby sulk" and "disgusted wince," saw in Il Duce's enthusiasm only a "semi-clownish tyrant" in "otherworldly" uniform. Where does this acerbity, something we have not recognized until this moment, originate? What factors account for this schoolgirl's cynicism?

As we learn later, not everyone in her family, one in which loyalty was valued more highly than any other virtue, shared in the refulgence of the day. Not everyone, it seems, was delighted by the ostentation of the pageantry and the display of the Italian *tricolore*. In fact, long before this extraordinary afternoon, Zaynab and Mariam's enrollment at the "Mussolini school" was, in some quarters of the family, quietly opposed. But surely this disagreement over schools or the sisters' featured role in the dictator's welcome wasn't responsible for Mariam's writerly paralysis? Even raising such a question recalls Mari Ruti's quandary in her Introduction to *The Offering*: "How am I to discuss this novel without giving away some of the plot elements that make it such a rewarding reading experience?" Her solution, reasonably enough, is to avoid the narrative and "stick to the story's emotional and existential resonances," and, for the most part, I will follow her lead. In a few instances, however, parsimony may be preferable to total avoidance, as unsatisfying as this miserly strategy might prove. So, I'll say this much: Something else *did* happen as a result of this eventful day. And nearly forty years after the Italian fascist's appearance in Benghazi, Mariam, buoyed by her husband's encouragement and moved by his entreaty, decides to confront the thing she has not written about or, rather, not *been able* to write about. One last crumb of information: this "thing," slowly revealed as the story progresses, is as beautifully described as it is painfully, and subtly, recounted.

"The Night Visitor" begins in similar fashion. On a lovely fall afternoon, Nausicaa Durand, a recent graduate of the Sorbonne who, a year before, successfully landed a teaching job at a high school in Paris's twelfth district, and her friend Pauline are "having a smoke" at their favorite café in the heart of *Quartier Latin*. In the midst of their conversation or, rather, in a brief respite in the middle of her peroration, Nausicaa stumbles toward an unsettling epiphany: "What am I doing? I'm actually discussing *him*. It's so weird." In fact, the story begins with a sense of the repetitive and compulsive quality of this weirdness, a strangeness linked to a deeply-felt emotion that immediately grabs her—and our—attention:

> *Poor Pauline: she just had to sit there and listen to me rehash the same story over and over again. I was in full monologue mode most of the time, I guess—out of fear; sheer visceral fear, the kind of gut-level dread I was trained to overcome.*

The novelette thus wastes little time casting its readers as intern psychoanalysts charged with identifying the multiple determinants of this compulsively reiterated monologue. That is to say, like the dreams Freud studied in *The Interpretation of Dreams* (1900), symptoms—Nausicaa's almost mechanical repetition and the affect accompanying it seem to indicate that it *is* a symptom—are typically *overdetermined*, driven into existence by numerous psychical factors. The anonymous "him" who invades her thoughts seems to play a featured role in her story, but who is he? And is he in any way referenced by the story's title, the "night visitor"? Is he the cause of Nausicaa's "gut-level dread"? If not, who or what is?

A few answers to these questions might prove helpful. The "*him*" to whom Nausicaa refers is an immensely talented Berber calligrapher named Madani. Nausicaa met him a year earlier on a mid-August holiday with Pauline on the Brittany coast where, along with another couple, they had been invited by their friend Tristan to gather at his parents' house to celebrate his graduation and birthday. Nausicaa's story moves quickly both to Madani and, curiously, to his impact on her sense of identity, an introspection noteworthy for both its adamant tone and seeming contradiction. A kind of ambiguity emerges that cannot be ignored. For although Nausicaa claims that he appeared "radically out of place" —"incongruous and unreal to the point of cognitive disconnection"—in the kitchen of Tristan's parents, she immediately tempers her observation, one made supremely ironic after the group is later treated to a superb meal Madani has prepared. But, at this point in her re-telling of the story, the kitchen and cuisine are hardly the issues:

> *Don't get me wrong, when I say he was out of place, I absolutely don't mean that with a racially biased connotation. Frankly, I tend to think of myself as having long outgrown the racism of my family.*

She declares herself a "post-racial woman," a catholic, socially progressive stance in which she takes great pride given the "ethnic uniformity of the environment" in which she was raised and the prejudice of her family.

This self-definition is quickly complicated by her staunch refusal "*to be held hostage to the imperatives of political correctness; not out of callous stubbornness, but because of the post-racial self-transformation I have been able to achieve over the years.*" This subjective ultimatum means, among other things, that she will neither countenance fatuity wherever it surfaces, nor tolerate its approbation. And when shortly after meeting him Madani spouts what she regards as blather, she reiterates her stance and rationalizes her adamance:

> *I am fully aware that I'm treading on thin ice here. But precisely because I am, and because I am a post-racial woman who refuses to be held hostage to the imperatives of political correctness, I feel compelled to speak courageously and candidly: regardless of what the calligrapher said, or whether he was aware of how much nonsense he was dishing out, what I found deeply problematic was the insincere air of quasi-beatitude with which everyone. . . greeted his comments.*

Everyone, that is, except she and Pauline. At this point of the story, the Berber calligrapher annoys Nausicaa, but at the same time also strikes at the core of her self-identity.

Gradually, however, her annoyance, even revulsion, subsides—and Madani's "tentacular hair," "in-your-face T-shirt," "clashing conservative earring," and generally "discordant oddness" are scarcely responsible for the change. Later, his "nonsense" is decoupled from the kitchen when, with a little help from his friends, he prepared "the most delicious" couscous Nausicaa had ever eaten; indeed, "*The food was so good a reverent hush over the table as we began to eat.*" Later that night just before retiring, and after enjoying a lively postprandial conversation and some good rum, Pauline and Nausicaa review the day, with Pauline urging her friend to recognize the depth and expressiveness of Madani's eyes, a depth that reveals pain and betrayal in his past. She was unmoved. But the following evening, after an unremarkable, but oddly affecting swim earlier in the day, a slideshow of Madani's art redeemed the evening and made it exceptional. She was stunned:

> *Madani's work is clearly more than an attempt to express consummate calligraphic virtuosity* . . . . *It's far more daring and ambitious than that as it seeks to chart unknown artistic territory, to open up esthetic and expressive avenues that stretch far beyond the trite, all-too-pat arabesque sensuality you find in the more conventional works of Arab calligraphy.*

This art, to Nausicaa's eye, was "*beautifully executed—a gorgeously choreographed dance of controlled chaos; the energy explosive and measured at once.*" It was a lot to consider, too much in fact; sleep came only after an animated exchange with Pauline about the art and her admiration of its intricacy and ingenuity.

And then there's a visitation in the middle of that night which requires more analysis than I can provide here. Again, my motive in withholding details of this incident should not be considered as evidence of my coyness. Rather, this "night visitor" is too intriguing, in some ways too fecund with implication, to be reduced to a sentence or two; further, an adumbration of the details might diminish the pleasure of discovering them.

What does *not* demand a scrupulous analysis are the moments in Benghazi" and "The Night Visitor" that paint detailed landscapes and cityscapes, skies and waters, and—foregrounded in both narratives—the imperfect workings of memory. Happily, these passages exist in such abundance that selecting representative examples requires little effort and poses even less danger of giving away too much of the stories' plots. Take, for example, Mariam's view of Benghazi's Market Square from her vantage point as a passenger on a bus stopped nearby:

> ... *the full-sized orange trees that marked off the red-brick court of our outdoor market stood as radiant as ever in their wooden planter boxes. Their immaculate leaves were treated with leaf shine, as usual, and the navel oranges glowed like lanterns in the blue-green foliage. Beyond those neatly spaced planters, there was the customary motley scene of our market: dazzling arrays of roses and flowers in florists' stands and the most amazing fruits and vegetables artfully arranged in the stalls and on the carts, their colors glistening, beckoning in the distance like the hypnotic hues of exotic porcelain novelties.*

Or Nausicaa's description of a late summer afternoon on the coast:

> *Mid-August in Brittany: a spectral touch of chill in the air; the faintest hint of autumnal crispness. Those intimations of fall in the sea breeze are as close as you can get to the idea of a beautiful melancholy—the spirit of autumn already looming in the crystal air, lazy plumes of mist rising from the western rim of that cellophane sky.*

These are two of many beautifully drawn instances in *Now and Then* from which readers will derive what Roland Barthes once called "the pleasure of the text."

That is to say, stunning evocations of place and time grace both stories: North African architecture and civic life, Breton landscapes and skies; familial interaction and intense affect; impeccable precision and bewildering ambiguity. As el Moncef foregrounds in *The Offering*, the woefully imperfect operations of memory, as I have suggested, are also depicted in these stories with similar care. As Nausicaa contemplates her first meeting Madani and interacting with him, for example, these deficiencies grow more apparent:

> *Strange how memory functions and malfunctions; how often we take its workings for granted. That it is selective is to be expected, of course; but when you find out the arcane mechanisms of recollection—the cutting and pasting, the highlighting and adumbrating, the deleting and inserting—*

So, while a reader's enjoyment of these stories might originate, as it does in the case of *The Offering*, in the thrill of sifting through evidence and navigating a character's frequently unreliable memory that muddles this evidence—and finally trying to identify the overdetermined sources of conflict in characters' troubled *inner* worlds—both "Benghazi" and "The Night Visitor" allow us numerous opportunities to luxuriate in the beauty of the external world el Moncef creates.

The beauty of this world, its natural beauty and that of the built environment, is also inextricably global—multinational and multicultural—as el Moncef insists in the two essays in *Now and Then*. Moreover, in these essays he translates into the vernacular of contemporary cultural theory the stakes of his fiction, especially the *psycho-political* consequences of tension between nations (Libya and Italy in "Benghazi") and ethnicities (Berber and French in "The Night Visitor"). This insistence could not be more urgently needed, as we stagger through yet another historical moment when national borders are being transformed into sites of political violence. As Anna Burns observes in *Milkman*: "'Political' of course covered anything to do with borders.... Any killing other than political and the community was in perplexity, also in anxiety, as to how to proceed." Set in Belfast during the Troubles, Burns's protagonist alludes here to the inurement of her neighbors to political murders at the boundary between Northern Ireland and the Republic of Ireland. Other borders are little different: those between Israel and Palestine, for example, or Russia and Ukraine. Salah el Moncef is acutely aware of this, of the tethering of chauvinistic nationalisms to sectarian and ethnic violence, and in "A Bridge Too Near: Détournement and the Promise of Transnational Conscience" he imagines a different reality and a different world. The essay is partly motivated by his noticing a large banner with the inscription "Aucun être humain n'est etranger sur cette terre" ("No human being is an alien on this earth") attached to the *"highly estheticized, highly theatricalized Le Pont des Arts—a bridge where amorous promises are exchanged between sweethearts and sealed with an inscribed "love lock."* The scores of "love locks" appended to the bridge are padlocks (the display of which is now prohibited) symbolizing lovers' commitment to each other; now, the loving troth symbolized by the locks has been replaced by *"nothing less than a solemn declaration launched in the heart of cosmopolitan Paris."* He continues:

> *In this context, one cannot help but recall Michael Ondaatje's "desired" new world and its borderless "cartography" through which people "become nationless" persons "walk[ing] upon ... an earth that [has] no maps."*

The implications of a borderless map are vast: thoroughly revised conceptions of nationhood, of citizenship, of conscience, and a vision of the possibilities of life together without xenophobia and racism.

Such a cartography also revises time. As such postcolonial theorists as Pheng Cheah argue in *What Is a World: On Postcolonial Literature as World Literature* (2016), the reimagining of new worlds entails more than physical or geographical spaces. For both el Moncef and Cheah, the privilege accorded spatiality in contemporary discussions of world literature (also world-making) and globalism too frequently occludes the idea, in Cheah's definition, that "*World*, however, is originally a temporal category. Before the world can appear as an object, it must first *be*" (2). Such an insistence also informs el Moncef's argument:

> *Announcing the birth of a world in which alienness is abrogated, the sign on the bridge seems to express similar aspirations: first, by redefining its appropriated site in terms of a new spatial index—the signifier of a nationless cartography; and second, by articulating it in relation to a new temporality—one that supersedes the passé romantic esthetic of the lovers' bridge . . . .*

What are the defining features of such a temporality? For Cheah, and among other things, it scrutinizes the opposition of linear time and its "mechanical causality" to the comparative openness of "teleological time." For el Moncef, borrowing a prospective focus from Frankfurt School philosopher Ernst Bloch, a revised temporality creates a *link between the here and now of a nation-centric world and the "not-yet" of a "global community" in which everyone becomes a citizen of one nation, the "earth."* This emphasis on the "not-yet-become," not on the past and the mythologies that sustain national history, is a foundation of Bloch's philosophy of hope, as it is for the inherent utopianism of el Moncef's essay. For intrinsic to this spatiotemporal renovation, this radical rethinking of mapping, is the commitment to engender a *"new correlation between transnationalism and the vision of a world of multiethnic coexistence."*

In such a transnational world, the alienated subjectivity to which el Moncef adverts in "The Voice of Exile," his retrospective view of *The Offering* with which *Here and Now* concludes, would cease to exist; that is, a figure like Tariq Abbassi, *"an intensified embodiment of the manifold symptoms of shock and dislocation experienced by the Maghrebi diaspora,"* would be rendered illegible as words like "dislocation" and "diaspora" would, in effect, lose some of their meaning. But because his is a decidedly national world where borders and boundaries are policed, Tariq's sense of liminality and "social-in-betweenness" is rooted in a larger *national* and *racial* "in-betweenness." The matter, however, is even more complicated and paradoxical than these few lines suggest, as el Moncef explains:

> *The story's potential for creating feelings of identification among diasporic readers of various identities brings us to another of Tariq's paradoxes: the fact that the symptoms of disjunction and homelessness that have contributed to the disintegration of the man's life are inextricably connected with the principles of tolerance, openness and global identification that have made him. . . the quintessential transnational subject. . . .*

The "transnational life," however difficult and at times impossible, is the only life Tariq wants to live, "*in spite of the ravages of racist hatred and violence.*" Another way of saying this is that a transnational subject with a truly cosmopolitan worldview will inevitably have to contend with the goose step of nationalism until a more transnational world can supersede it.

Until then, characters like Tariq, Mariam, and Nausicaa will carry with them scars from the worlds in which they live. One metaphor for these signs of past injury, manifested in very different ways in these characters' lives, is what Paul Ricouer in his grand opus *Memory, History, Forgetting* (2004) calls an inscription. "Inscription" connotes a range of engravings, from tattoos to the "get well wish" on the envelope Mariam receives from her husband, from signs on bridges to faint etchings on a waxy substrate of memory that Freud compared to a "mystic writing pad." The global, nation-less cartography el Moncef imagines does possess, at least in some mild sense, a spatial marking, but it also possesses a more profound temporal dimension. Ricouer finds such markings the "most problematic but the most significant" to our internal lives because they signal "the passive persistence of first impressions: an event has struck us, touched us, affected us, and the affective mark remains in our mind" (427). Salah el Moncef explores these marks with both wisdom and elegance in *Now and Then*.

Provost Professor Stephen Watt
University of Indiana Bloomington
April 2022

Benghazi

For Gilda, who inspired this story,
and for Maha, who willed it

And she learned the arts of eloquence and writing, calculus, horse riding, and bravery ... And she learned all the handicrafts of men and women until she became unique in her epoch.
>—"Nur al-Din and Mariam the Sash Maker"
>(*One Thousand and One Nights*, 1836 Arabic edition)

Why do you not as well our battles fight,
And wear our armor? Suffer this, and then
Let all the world be topsy-turvèd quite.
>—Elizabeth Cary, *The Tragedy of Mariam, the Fair Queen of Jewry*

Map of Benghazi

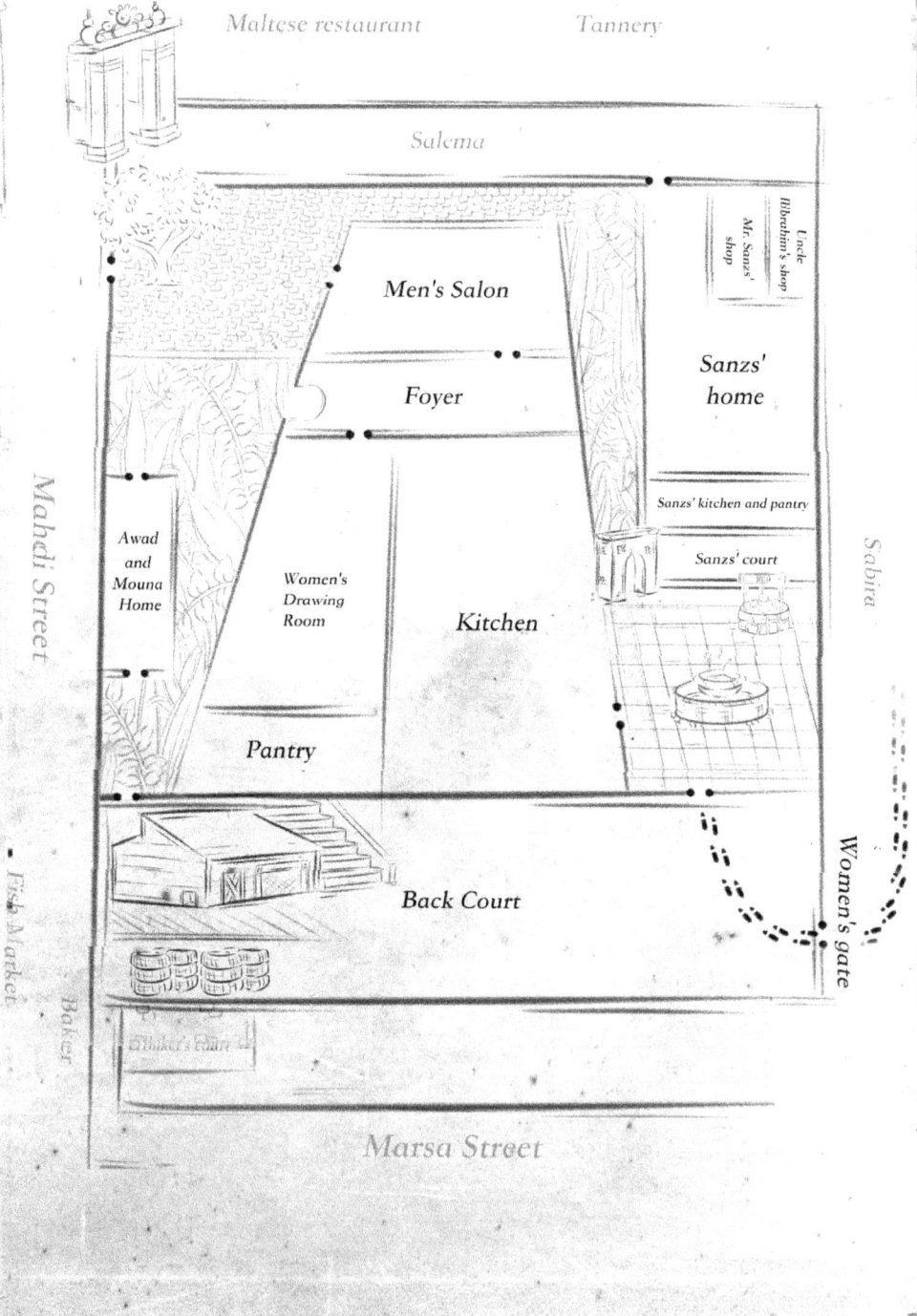

List of Characters

Mariam Khaldoon Family

*Father: Ahmad Khaldoon,
a Benghazian of Andalusian descent*

*Mother: Noor Akram,
an Alexandrine of Turkish descent*

*Father's maternal uncle: Ibrahim Mahdi ("Uncle Ibrahim"),
native of Benghazi and former mayor of Benghazi*

Khaldoon children

*Muhammad
Ali
Zaynab
Mariam*

*"Uncle Awad" Damanhuri (in charge of security at Khaldoon home)
"Auntie Mouna" Damanhuri (his wife and Khaldoon housekeeper)
Antar Damanhuri (their son)*

*Esther and Saul Sanz: Khaldoon family tenants
Mr. Fribourg: Ahmad Khaldoon business partner*

Mariam and Zaynab's teachers

*Signora Taramelli
Signora Cabrini
Signora Cordini*

Preface

Set in 1930s Benghazi, the cosmopolitan Libyan city perched on the Mediterranean, Salah el Moncef's dazzling novella transports us to a time right before the Second World War, when Mussolini's boot presses oppressively on Libya's throat, suffocating the country's anticolonial and antifascist sentiments. Narrated from the perspective of an adolescent girl, Mariam Khaldoon, the novella weaves a complex mesh of conceptual connections between the authoritarian rule of a colonizing dictator and—the far less menacing yet still disconcerting—authoritarian rule of a family patriarch, between Mussolini and Mariam's father, the successful business owner Mr. Khaldoon. I do not mean to imply that Mr. Khaldoon is anything like Mussolini: quite the contrary, it is his deep hatred of Mussolini, whose political views he explicitly resists, that causes Mr. Khaldoon to withdraw from his family, particularly from Mariam and her older sister, Zaynab. More specifically, what torments and alienates Mr. Khaldoon is that the Italian school attended by his daughters chooses the two girls to greet Mussolini on behalf on their school during the dictator's visit to Benghazi. However, from Mariam's young point of view, Mr. Khaldoon's power over her is as seamless as that of Mussolini over Libya. The situation is made all the more perplexing by the fact that Mariam regards her father as a reasonable man who deserves her love and respect (whereas Mussolini is an unreasonable persecutor who is despised by everyone in the family).

Mr. Khaldoon is distant and detached from his daughters even before Mussolini's visit. Yet he is not a tyrant: despite his profound distaste for all things related to fascism, he has struck a compromise with his wife, who believes in the importance of educating Mariam and Zaynab, by allowing them to attend the Italian "Mussolini school." However, the brief exchange between the dictator and his daughters breaks his spirit, causing him to retreat even more than before into his study within the men's quarters of the family residence. Although Mariam's contact with him has, prior to this rupture, been limited to Friday morning visits to his study—visits carefully curated and mediated by her mother—she feels the loss of this already limited avenue of communication deeply, not being able to understand why her father is so upset yet vaguely aware that his frustration and depression are caused by her fleeting interaction with Mussolini. It is as if, without meaning to—after all, she did not ask to be her school's ambassador in relation to Mussolini—she has betrayed her loyalty to her father and her family, a loyalty that is the glue that has until then held the family unit together. On some level, then, Moncef's novella is about a girl's attempt to navigate the treacherous terrain between love and fear, affection and remorse, in relation to her remote father.

As an adolescent girl, Mariam does not fully grasp the brutality of Mussolini. For her, he is a cartoonish character whose pomp she mocks with Zaynab from a distance even as she is also terrified when compelled to talk to him. Unfortunately, she is also terrified to talk to her father. All she wants is his affection, which means that she feels his disapproval keenly, even if this disapproval remains largely unspoken. Indeed, what makes matters even harder is that her father's intense aversion to her meeting with Mussolini remains profoundly enigmatic to her. In this sense, the psychoanalytic concept of enigmatic signifiers—developed by Jacques Lacan and Jean Laplanche—seems to accurately capture Mariam's side of the affective dynamic between her and her father. Enigmatic signifiers are opaque messages emitted by other people that are derailing because they remain inaccessible and indecipherable. Their power over children and adolescents is especially formidable because children and adolescents do not necessarily possess the cognitive capacity to fully make sense of the adult world. They are routinely left wondering what adults mean, what they want, and why they want what they appear to want. The attempt to please an adult who transmits enigmatic signifiers, and who therefore remains unreadable and mysterious, can be utterly disorientating; it generates an inexplicable sense of restlessness and overagitation. No wonder Mariam has trouble sleeping at night. Enigmatic signifiers create a painful intersection between seduction and rejection, and this intersection is where Mariam finds herself trapped: her desire for her father's approval is repeatedly met with a dismissal that is unintelligible in not having a clear cause.

Mariam's father is a formidable presence even in his absence—perhaps precisely due to his absence. He dictates what Mariam is and is not allowed to do through her mother. However, more than anything, it is his detachment that causes her to feel irrelevant. It is, then, fitting that Moncef's novella contains only one scene where Mariam interacts with her father in person: a masterful depiction of one of her Friday morning visits to his study. Mariam is not permitted to speak to her father directly unless explicitly invited to do so. It is her mother who tells her father about her achievements at school, about how her teachers have praised her as "a highly gifted" and "precocious" pupil, and about a poem she has written. Pleased by her naïvely nationalist poem, which Mariam is asked to recite for him, Mr. Khaldoon proudly exclaims: "*Mashallah*, Mariam! *Brahwa!*"

Uncannily—and this is perhaps the most obvious way in which Moncef draws a cautious analogy between Mr. Khaldoon and Mussolini—this endorsement echoes that of Mussolini, who states "*Brava*, Miriam, *brava*" after she hands him the gift that her school has chosen for him: a pair of elaborately embroidered black-and-gold slippers. Although Mussolini mispronounces her name, she is pleased by the notoriety that his using it grants her, especially after he fails to remember Zaynab's name when thanking her for the greeting that Zaynab reads, in perfect Italian, from an index card. Although Mariam is proud of Zaynab's excellent Italian, hearing the dictator signal her out by calling her by her name makes her feel special—which is precisely how she would like to feel in relation to her father but never does. Indeed, at the end of the novella, Mariam recalls that her father stating "*Mashallah*, Mariam! *Brahwa!*" in response to her poem was the only time he ever said her name. That this sole utterance of her name by her father replicates Mussolini's praise creates an uncomfortable correspondence between the two men.

The parallels between Mussolini and Mr. Khaldoon—not in terms of their political views but in terms of the cryptic power that the two men wield—are evident from Mariam's depiction of the atmosphere of her father's study during the visit when she is asked to recite her poem:

> The head of our family sat in his armchair like a monarch, beneath that most emblematic symbol of protection: his beloved damascene silver plate, adorning the wall with a hamsa sign at its center. . . . I don't remember how long we spoke, but I can clearly visualize how humbly satisfied I was: just glad to be sitting there before Father, contemplating the distant glow of his barely contained pride—the tentative warmth of his oblique gaze, the uplifting power of his indirect words.

Mr. Khaldoon's authority is here depicted as being more benign than that of Mussolini: a form of protection—even of a "barely contained pride," "tentative warmth," and "uplifting power"—rather than of tyranny. Yet at the end of the novella, the adult Mariam reflects on this authority as follows: "I never really thought of an alternative to the way he was—the way things were in those days for a father and his daughter—but it would be dishonest to say that those Friday glimpses of Father had never left me with a nameless sense of incompletion, or even emptiness perhaps." That the incompletion and emptiness that Mariam refers to is linked to "namelessness" is significant, given the weightiness that Mariam attributes to the instances when she is startled to hear Mussolini and her father pronounce her name. We know that Mr. Khaldoon would have been genuinely horrified by any analogy between himself and Mussolini. Yet this analogy is impossible to avoid and, ultimately, revolves around the power that the two men possess with regard to making another person feel noteworthy by the simple act of calling them by their name.

Moncef thus presents a compelling portrait of how authoritarian men elicit the desire for approval in those over whom they hold power, Mussolini on the level of the nation and Mr. Khaldoon on the level of the family. In both cases, it is the aloof unapproachability of the men in question that constitutes a large part of their power. The novella contains several psychologically intricate depictions of Mariam's relationships with women: her beautiful mother whose affection is palpable even if it feels somewhat precarious and capricious; the gorgeous and self-confident fortuneteller, Markunda, who predicts a beautiful future for Mariam and offers her talismans that are supposed to protect her for the rest of her life; and the maternal, solicitous housekeeper Auntie Mouna, who is sincerely remorseful after having accidentally hit Mariam in the mouth with her washboard. Mariam's (only slightly older) brother Ali comes across as mercurial and gregarious. In contrast, the two adult male members of the Khaldoon family, Mr. Khaldoon and Mariam's oldest brother, Muhammad—who inherits his father's position as the family patriarch when the latter suddenly dies at the age of forty-five—are portrayed as affectively distant and hard to read. They are the epitome of men who wield power—"hold forth," to borrow a phrase from Roland Barthes—at the same time as they withhold attention and approval from those who desperately seek it.

Yet, interestingly, the adult Mariam acknowledges that there was something about the dynamic between her and her father that was also beyond his control, that had a logic that transcended both of them. As she states:

> It was always as if the entire experience had a certain power—independent of either of us—to make me feel helpless and small before this one irrepressible realization: the wordless awareness that although our Friday hour was so dearly desired, there was something about the space in which it took place that I found impossible to accept—a physical force, maybe, that invested the whole room with a primal power of impingement entirely detached from his personal beliefs or volition; a mute, relentless agency acting like a harsh and hostile environment fraught with elemental properties that were fundamentally toxic for both of us—as alien and unnatural to both our beings as the deep sea is to the novice diver.

On the one hand, Mariam finds it impossible to accept the "primal power of impingement" that infused the space of the Friday meetings; on the other, she recognizes that the power in question had little to do with her father's personal beliefs or volition, that it was a matter of an impersonal agency that did not represent her father's intimate inclinations or attitudes but rather epitomized the unfolding of intergenerational customs that were harsh, hostile, and "toxic" to both her and her father. It is as if Mr. Khaldoon's power was primarily structural in nature. It also perfectly exemplified one of the main arguments of deconstructive feminism, namely that patriarchal power does not benefit anyone: it may hurt men less than women but ultimately it is toxic to both; it delimits both, curtailing the affective range of both men and women, in this case the fragile relationship between father and daughter.

Moncef accentuates this point by portraying Mr. Khaldoon, outside of his relationship with his daughters, as a sophisticated, intelligent, and flourishing businessman with admirable religious, political, and ethical attitudes. He practices a tolerant and pacifist form of Sufism. He is a staunch opponent of fascism and a supporter of political freedom. His business practices are openminded, revealing a benevolent attitude toward cultures other than his own, for he trades, among other countries, with Egypt, Sudan, Ceylon, China, Ethiopia, and Yemen. He is friendly with Maltase and Moroccan business owners on his street. And he trusts all his banking affairs to a French Jewish merchant, Monsieur Fribourg. Upon Monsieur Fribourg's recommendation, he is even willing to help the Jewish Sanz family, persecuted by the fascists, by offering them housing in the annex of his family compound. His charitable openness in running his business and his antifascist political views contrast starkly with his authoritarian relationship with his daughters.

The ending of Moncef's novella—which I quoted above—suggests that this contrast has less to do with Mr. Khaldoon personally than with historical forces that have shaped the relationship between fathers and daughter for generations, forces that neither party is able to escape. This is the main familial tragedy of Moncef's text—a text where national and global tragedies are hinted at but remain in the margins. It is also a theme with universal ramifications in the sense that a historically dictated dissociation between fathers and daughters seems to be a common predicament across many cultures. The theme certainly spoke to me as the daughter of an emotionally distant father who grew up in an otherwise gender-egalitarian Nordic country.

It is unclear from the novella whether the man Mariam ends up marrying reproduces the emotional dynamic she has with her father or whether, instead, it comes closer to the warm and playful relationship that she has with her brother Ali. My hope is that the novel that Moncef writes from the rich foundations of his novella will answer this question, along with other mysteries that the novella gestures toward, such as the fate of the Sanz family. In a sense, the entire novella could be said to represent an enormous enigmatic signifier, this time in the best possible sense of the term: an evocative, somewhat secretive piece of writing that elicits the reader's desire for more. Precisely because all is not revealed, because not all the plot elements are tidily tied up—we do not, for instance, know how Mariam and her husband (who is he anyway?) end up in Bloomington, Indiana—we want to know more: we are eager to see the rest of the story unfold. In this manner, Moncef, in a clever rhetorical move, places us, his readers, structurally in the same affective predicament as Mariam: we want more, though this time the person who withholds what we covet is not an authoritarian father but rather a gifted writer who understands that desire is a function of lack.

By choosing an adolescent narrator and by setting the bulk of the novella in the pre-war years, Moncef is able to capture a moment in history when Mussolini can still be mocked, and when an analogy between Mussolini and Mr. Khaldoon is still possible because Mussolini's monstrosity has not yet been fully revealed. Yet the looming war already casts a threatening shadow over the Khaldoon family. In addition, because the novella moves back and forth in time, at the beginning of the story, after the preface in 1970s Indiana where we briefly meet the adult Mariam with her professor husband, we find Mariam in 1942—in the middle of the Second World War, when Benghazi is in the grip of the Fascists and the Nazis—being left in charge of the family compound by Muhammad and Ali. We know that the young men are headed to Alexandria but we do not know why; we do not know why they are leaving the fifteen-year-old Mariam in charge. All we know is that she is unusually skilled in handling firearms and that the political situation, particularly for Benghazi's Jewish residents, is urgent: the names of Mr. and Mrs. Sanz have been placed on the list affixed to the door of Slat Lekbira, the main synagogue in Benghazi, indicating that they are expected to make preparations for being sent to a concentration camp.

The World Holocaust Remembrance Center, Yad Vashem, reports that at the eve of the Second World War, there were over 30,000 Jews in Libya, whereas now there are none. Many left the country after the war due to repeated persecution. But the war had already taken its toll. Between the end of 1940 and the beginning of 1943—exactly when Mariam is left in charge of the Khaldoon family compound—the Cyrenaica region of Libya, and especially Benghazi, was a site of constant fighting between Italian and German troops on the one hand and British ones on the other. During periods when the Italians or the Germans were in charge, Jews were shipped to concentration camps in Europe and Libya, including the infamous Jado camp in Libya. Every two weeks, the fascist occupants posted in synagogues lists of families who were expected to get ready to leave for the feared death camps.

This is the heartrending moment in time when Moncef's novella begins, with the Khaldoon family trying to rescue the Sanz family from deportation after their names have been posted. As Ali says to Mariam:

> Do *not* get worked up, sister, not now. Sergeant Saeed knows and is watching out, Antar knows and is watching out, Uncle Ibrahim knows and is watching out. Everybody in the neighborhood is on the lookout. More importantly, we do have a getaway solution for them. We just need Uncle Kareem to help us with our solution when we get to Alexandria. Trust me, by the time we get back, the Sanzes' troubles will be over. We just need to help them lay low for a few days.

Sergeant Saeed, a former officer in the Egyptian army, is Auntie Mouna's husband. Antar is their son. Uncle Ibrahim is Mr. Khaldoon's business partner. One gets the sense of feverish organizing not merely on the part of the Khaldoon family but of the entire neighborhood to rescue the Sanz family. Uncle Kareem, Mrs. Khaldoon's cousin in Alexandria, is in the business of importing and exporting luxury goods, so presumably he has the necessary connections to get the Sanz family out of Libya. The Khaldoon family is helping them lay low until this becomes possible. It may even be that Muhammad and Ali are on their way to Alexandria to organize the rescue operation at that end. But here the narrative tantalizingly breaks off. As I noted, we do not know where the brothers are headed. Nor do we know what happens to the Sanz family or whether or not Mariam is forced to use the family's Walther pistol that Ali gives her before leaving for Alexandria. For the rest of this intense storyline, we need to wait for Moncef to turn his novella into a novel.

There are two more stylistic aspects of the novella that I want to briefly address in this preface. The first is Moncef's marvelous dexterity in bringing his characters to life with just a few schematic, impressionistic phrases, as he does, for instance, with Markunda:

> She wore the traditional indigo turban deliberately loose to show off her pleasing countenance, her raven hair, and the marvelous Tuareg-cross earrings she wore. . . . Her eyes were the first thing I noticed as I studied her face: the aquamarine luminescence of those eyes contrasted strangely with the copper glow of her flushed cheeks, and the strangeness was ineffably compelling, haunting beyond words.

This striking woman, who immediately takes control of the situation when she spots Mariam and her mother in the middle of the turf-covered town square, contrasts humorously with her clumsy and uncomfortable husband who is left awkwardly holding the reigns of their two unruly camels on the road while his wife briskly strides toward Mariam and her mother to read Mariam's fortune.

Consider, also, the depiction of the orderly who admits Mariam to the infirmary after Auntie Mouna has accidently split her lip with her washboard: "He was the same mysterious man I would notice every now and then outside the infirmary—a gaunt, chain-smoking, tobacco-skinned Sicilian who wore an outsize lab coat, a precarious comb-over, and bottle-bottom glasses that obscured his gaze and gave him a deceptively sinister air." The novella is filled with such brief yet evocative depictions, so that even minor characters, such as the orderly, are skillfully drawn as compelling portraits. Appropriately enough, given the aloof nature of Mariam's father, he gets as brief a delineation as the two relatively minor characters I have just mentioned: "his sphinxian features, half Andalusian, half Phoenician, tightly framed by that perpetual scarlet fez; his black beard as dense and even as steel wool; his nose proud and elegant and straight, like the exquisite barb of an arrow carved out of sandalwood." In this one stunning sentence, Moncef manages to portray the enigmatic gist of Mariam's indecipherable father. It is precisely Moncef's extraordinary ability to paint minute portraits of both his characters and the general atmosphere within which these characters move, along with his equally extraordinary ability to compose a compelling plot, that sets him apart as a uniquely gifted writer.

The second—related—stylistic aspect of the novella I want to call attention to is the scintillating manner in which Moncef describes the city of Benghazi, which, thanks to his elaborate representations, becomes one of the novella's main "characters": a living and breathing entity that commands the reader's attention as absorbingly as Mariam and the rest of the Khaldoon family. It is in fact in his exquisite portraiture of Benghazi that Moncef's prose reaches the apex of its luminosity; when he depicts Benghazi, he writes with a lyrical virtuosity that causes his elegant sentences to sparkle as brightly as Benghazi's rooftops in sunlight:

> We had not been there more than a few minutes when the sun broke out from behind the clouds, just as it began to slip below the roofline of Palazzo Prosdocimo. The metamorphic, amber glow of that lowering sun had suddenly transmogrified the entire east side of the square, muted its daunting architectural grandeur into a chiaroscuro scene of enchantment: our Art Deco Municipal Theater—the marmoreal monumentalism of its

ice-white rectangular planes and its blind arcade of stilted arches shifting to a grisaille of dark ginger root and burnt umber; the imposing sandstone façade of the Military Association—pilasters receding into the shadows like half-melted wax tablets; the avenue of slender palm trees along Viale della Stazione stretching out to the eastern horizon in soft, paper-cut silhouette. All of it already fading as fast as a chimera thanks to the treacherous transience of our desert afterglow.

This is poetry as prose, prose as poetry. The novella is replete with such vibrant, iridescent depictions of the city which animate the text at key moments and which force the reader to pause to admire the sheer splendor of the text. It would be difficult to imagine Moncef's narrative without the backdrop of Benghazi, which manages to glisten at the same time as it is a dusty, bustling, and humming beehive of activity.

Structurally, the novella is organized around one eventful day in the young Mariam's life: to her utter dismay, she is told by Auntie Mouna that her farther has forbidden her from accompanying Zaynab on her Wednesday outings to invite the prominent women of the neighborhood to Mrs. Khaldoon's tea parties; Auntie Mouna accidentally hits her in the mouth with her washboard; her mother, Auntie Mouna, Ali, and Antar accompany Mariam to the infirmary where she gets her lip fixed; and Markunda reads her fortunate, promising her a wonderful future. Around this day, the story fans in a number of directions, the most prominent of which are Mussolini's visit; the depiction of how the Khaldoon family runs its business, with the women participating in preparing the luxurious fabrics they sell in their store; and—importantly—Mariam's Friday morning visit to her father's study. The story is bookended by brief fragments that reveal that it is Mariam who has written the story and that she plans to complete it by writing a second half, just as Moncef plans to complete his novella by turning it into a novel. The first new segment to be added seems to be about the Sanz family moving into the Khaldoon's annex about a year before Mr. Khaldoon's death and a year and a half before the start of the war. As I have noted, there are a fair number of loose ends that will presumably be addressed in the completed work. Yet the novella can be read on its own without the loss of any of the story's splendor.

Mari Ruti, Distinguished Professor
University of Toronto
Newfoundland,
April 2022

When we had finished our Sacher torte and drunk our coffee, Basil rose to his feet and told me to wait. Just as I reached for my tote, starting to stand up myself, he said, "Stay put, my love. I'll be right back."

He pulled a blue envelope out of his inside jacket pocket and walked off toward the door, gone in a fraction of a second. And so, I had no choice but to remain seated and wait—my hand still on my bag, my mind slightly numb with surprise; trying to settle back into the cushioned, wrought-iron chair as unclumsily as possible; trying to settle into the new reality of Basil's vanishing act.

It wasn't a comfortable wait. Our marble-topped two-seater was beginning to take on that sad, trashed air of vacated café tables. When my edgy eyes locked with the waitress's, I felt obliged to give her a guilty smile from my awkward solitary corner—in apology for this inopportune hiatus before the check. She beamed back at me with a playfully commiserative look in her eyes, as if to say, *I wonder what your husband is up to this time!*

And I just sat there and waited—watching time drip and dribble away moment by moment, pondering my options as the seconds ticked by. There was a pocket edition of the *Rubaiyat* in my tote. I took it out, opened it at random, and began to read, my eyes fidgeting between Khayyám's verse and the door through which Basil had vanished with his secret in his hand.

Endless minutes of restless reading. Then, just as I started to lose patience, my mercurial husband came back in, striding briskly across the carpeted room toward our little out-of-the-way alcove. With a broad smile on his playful mischief-maker face, he sat down opposite me again, as if no interruption had intervened between us, and held out that strange pastel-blue envelope.

I tossed the book back into my bag and took his envelope. It felt a bit bulky as I unsealed it—there was a bulging card inside. Carefully, I laid the envelope on the table and pulled the card out among the remains of our twosome coffee klatch. A *get-well wish* was inscribed in gold capital letters on the China-blue cover. With my right hand, I pressed the message side of the card flat on the table, and with my left, I flipped it open, revealing a Parker fountain pen inside. I lifted the pen and read Basil's note:

Part One of your story is beautiful and deeply compelling. Translating it gave me so much joy! Why must your adoring husband's work sit in a drawer? Why must your work remain unfinished? I know I've asked you this question before, and you told me writing it was rough going all along—and "a bit sickening," you added. I don't know how to take that, the "sickening" part. One way to deal with the sickness of the past would be to assume that some things that make us sick now are essential to our definitive healing in the long run. Please finish your amazing story, and I will proudly translate the rest with as much delight as I translated Part One.

P.S. The elderly lady who has just sold me the Parker in the gift shop told me she had been seeing us at the Silver Spoon for years. "You always look so wonderful together," she said. "The picture-perfect couple." She was very nice—said you looked like Samantha Eggar and meant it as a big compliment.

I looked up from the card and gazed at my husband in silence, in a mix of amazement and gratitude. He handed me the presentation box across the table, grinning proudly, like a man who had finalized a satisfying deal.

Later, when we got home, I sat down in my study to try out the new pen. I filled it with ink, grabbed a writing pad, put both pen and paper on the desk, and leaned back in my chair.

He's right, I thought. *This is probably the best time to do it—finish what I started*. It was 1976, and the summer would be brimming with beautiful signs and symbols for millions of us. Basil's work was going very well in the Comp Lit Department. He was writing a great book, and his colleagues loved us. The Bloomington spring had hit the hills around town—swift, as usual, wild, and disarranging. The cherry trees nodded with the mad blossoming of April, and we were all rooting for Jimmy Carter, at least in this part of Indiana. The future looked bright and beautiful. There was no better time than now to talk about the past—that other spring, and the roiling years that led up to it.

I opened the desk drawer, pulled out Part One of the manuscript—the translated version—as if I wanted to prove to myself that I was willing to acknowledge my husband's commitment to my work. I commenced reading his translation . . .

Part One

It was the spring Ali decided I was old enough to be entrusted with the security of our mother's home.

"From now on, you're the man of the house, so to speak," my brother said. "Actually, as soon as we roll out of the courtyard," he corrected himself with a wink. "Here, take it. It's yours. You've earned it."

Ali held out the Beretta, and in his huge palm, it looked toy-like and diminutive. The twinkle in his eyes was a strange mix of paternal pride and teenage pranksterism. I took it and put it in the pocket of my safari jacket—the practice coat he had bought for me in Alexandria.

"When are you leaving?" I asked.

"After tomorrow at the crack of dawn. The trip to end all trips! We're going to milk this lull in the fighting for all it's worth, sister. It's going to be good for business and good for our neighbors. Are you nervous already? Where's the toughness you told me about? Has it deserted you already?"

Ali's playful green eyes crackled with bantering mischief—my brother's way of managing *his* nervousness.

"What are you talking about? *I'm* not nervous. I know your guns in and out. I'm your gun cleaner, for heaven's sake. You even let me clean the Winchester once, didn't you?"

"And a fine job you did, too. And now you've fired your first live rounds, and we know you're a natural—what more could you want? Actually, we won't really know before you've tried the Walther. Are you excited?"

"Of course I am—you know that. But as I said, I clean them up, I take care of them, I dry fire some of them. I know your guns through and through. You don't have to worry."

"I'm not worried. I know I can trust you fully. That's why I'm giving you this with the Beretta."

He pulled a box of ammunition out of the pocket of his bomber jacket, waved it before me with a teasing grin.

"A whole box?" I gasped.

"Yes, and I know you're going to use it responsibly. Hide it well inside the house, but keep it within easy reach for yourself. You have to show me where you're going to hide it. While I'm away, all safety rules still apply. No changes whatsoever. Dummy rounds and dry firing by yourself. Blanks and target balloons with Sergeant Saeed. Live once a week with Sergeant Saeed—now that you've got your own live bullets."

Sergeant Saeed—Sergeant Happy in Arabic—was my brothers' nickname for our house guard. The sergeant—my sister and I called him Uncle Awad—came from Damietta and used to be a gunnery officer in the Egyptian army before he joined us. He had a number of firearms in his home and had taught my father and two brothers everything they knew about weapons. His military days were long behind him, though, and he now dressed very much like most men from northern Egypt: in a traditional galabia and caftan with those huge, wide sleeves, and a scarlet tarboosh with a white turban wound around its rim. The erstwhile Egyptian soldier who guarded our house was quite literally the living image of the "man from the Nile Delta"—the tall, traditionally clad stock character you see in practically every Egyptian movie from the fifties. There was never any variation in the way he dressed, except for two things: in the hot months, he traded his turban and tarboosh for a snow-white skullcap, and in the cold months, he topped his galabia and caftan with a russet-brown camel-hair *binish*, the time-honored Egyptian overcoat. Uncle Awad lived with his family in a small annex in our front courtyard. His wife, Mouna—we called her Auntie Mouna—helped Mother with household chores, and his teenage son, Antar, ran our errands.

My brother remained silent for a long, uncomfortable moment, the expression on his face altered with an all-too-sudden, all-too-unusual look of sad gravity. The sun was going down fast behind Municipio, the city hall building, and the livid shadows of early evening began to descend on the back court like smoke. Our black-and-white target stood as if suspended in the shadow of the north wall, its rusty frame invisible against the dark mass of the tire backstop. There were noises of kitchen clatter behind the wall separating us from the house patio. Dinnertime approaching.

He leaned toward me and said, "I can trust you with these deadly weapons, sister, can't I?" The amber starbursts around his pupils were like streaks of luminescence converging toward the pitch-black center of his intelligent eyes.

"That's absolutely right," I replied. "You can trust me."

With his eyes still fixed on me, he pointed back over his shoulder toward the outside stairs and the rooftop laundry room. That laundry room was the highest point of our house.

He said, "The binoculars, Mariam. Will you remember what I told you?"

"I know the rules by heart, brother."

"I know, but I want you to repeat them for me just the same."

"Use them upstairs inside the laundry room only. Always keep them in their case. Don't let anybody see them. Never lean outside the laundry room windows when using them. Keep at a safe distance from the laundry room windows. And last but not least, when observing with the binoculars, don't be excessively nosy: stay focused on the harbor, the docks, and the piers from the north window and Piazza del Municipio from the south window. You don't have to worry about me, Ali."

"I'm not worried," he said.

He was worried, though, about his fifteen-year-old sister. It was the spring of '42, and Benghazi, once again under Mussolini's Fascist regime, was turning into an exponentially dangerous city where burglary, kidnapping, and even murder were becoming commonplace. I asked him about Esther and Saúl Sanz, our tenants.

"Muhammad spoke with Mr. Sanz at length, and Mr. Sanz spoke with his wife. We told him the Fascists had put up this week's deportation list on the door of Slat Lekbira Synagogue—their names were on it. He said he wouldn't tell Mrs. Sanz—it was enough aggravation for him already."

Ali saw the worried look on my face, and he leaned toward me again, speaking in a whisper, slowly and deliberately.

"Do *not* get worked up, sister, not now. Sergeant Saeed knows and is watching out. Antar knows and is watching out. Uncle Ibrahim knows and is watching out. Everybody in the neighborhood is on the lookout. More importantly, we do have a getaway solution for them. We just need Uncle Kareem to help us with our solution when we get to Alexandria. Trust me, by the time we get back, the Sanzes' troubles will be over. We just need to help them lie low for a few days."

⁂

The next day Ali gave me the Walther, and I had my second target shoot with live ammunition.

This time Muhammad and Uncle Awad were there, and when I was done demonstrating my skills with the weapon, there was a long silence during which only Ali was beaming—the deeply satisfied grin of a proud, contented instructor presenting an exceptional pupil.

Muhammad walked up to the target and studied it gravely. We crowded around him, waiting for the verdict. When he spoke, he raised his index finger and looked in Uncle Awad's direction, as if the flawless demonstration was his work.

"Astounding marksmanship," he declared. "You have my blessings, as long as everything is conducted with circumspection—under Sergeant Saeed's supervision, of course."

Our older brother's understated but intense physical presence was the diametrical opposite of Ali's trim and tall elegance, his restless energy and winsome trickster's eyes. Our family head had the same compact Andalusian build as our father; the same short, go-getter, muscular efficiency; the same prominent martial brow glowing above his steady, black eyes like burnished bronze. Muhammad's short crop of curly black hair hugged his oval head like a protective coat of steel wool. When he made a fist, his hand looked like a sledgehammer. The precocious leader of our family. Forced by fate and circumstances to assume a paternalistic seriousness beyond his twenty years.

Later, when I showed Ali where I was going to hide the weapons, he sensed my misgivings about our brother's reaction. He spoke as much in defense of Muhammad as to reassure me. "He *is* very impressed, believe me. He's also very, very proud of you. He just feels that he needs to appear . . . sort of aloof and neutral. I guess he feels he's become the head of the family a bit too soon. Your new responsibility reminds him of his. Also, he thinks he always has to appear serious—you know, to make up for Father's . . . you know . . . absence."

✻

Father's absence.

The word we never dared to use always lurked behind our family euphemism like a nameless kernel of pain—the ghost of an unforgettable fracture buried deep in our bones, a throbbing wedge of rage lodged in the depths of our being.

The death date we never forgot, and the terrible manner of his death—a good man overtaken by the end in the unlikeliest place, alone and helpless in the beloved wholesale store that had been his livelihood since he was a teenager.

✻

Father died of a heart attack on March 25, 1939. It was his uncle who found him—the man we all called Uncle Ibrahim. He had dropped in at the wholesale store for a chat and discovered Father in one of the storage rooms, slumped facedown over a bag of coffee. He passed away four days after I turned twelve, and so I found myself orphaned at the same age he had been. The wedding of my sister, Zaynab, had been planned for the summer of 1941. He didn't live to give her away. She was fifteen; he, forty-five.

Up until that day, we had been an ordinary, progressive Benghazi family—shaped by the universal love, tolerance, and pacifism of our faith (we are deeply secretive, blindly committed Sufis), still capable of leading a peaceful, uncomplicated life in spite of all the horrid things Mussolini's Fascists had done to our country. We lived on Mahdi Street—a stone's throw away from the most beautiful harbor and the most beautiful fish market in the world, two doors down from Ibrahim Mahdi, the celebrated marksman, the fabled mystical leader, and the providential uncle who became like a father to our father when he was orphaned. By the time Father had turned fifteen, they were trade associates, with the two men's names elegantly printed on their business stationery and envelopes—Ibrahim Mahdi and Ahmad Khaldoon. The two importers ran a prosperous company out of the nineteenth-century Ottoman building affectionately called "the Whale"—that gigantic Shasheer Street wholesale store inherited by our father and his mother upon our grandfather's death.

By the time the twenties came around, the names of the two men who operated out of the Whale had become locally synonymous with high-quality imports and fine exotic products. Within a few years, they had managed to build an excellent business reputation, importing coffee from Yemen and Ethiopia, tea from Ceylon and China, spices and textiles from everywhere. Their main trading partner was Mother's cousin Kareem Akram, a big import/export merchant and head of a company operating out of Alexandria, Egypt.

Once every spring, Father and Uncle Ibrahim would charter a bus from the Benghazi school district, load up one of the company trucks with food and barbecue meat, and take the Mahdi and Khaldoon families to the Green Mountain for a barbecue picnic at

Cyrene, the ancient Greek and Roman city near present-day Shahhat. I have the fondest memories of those picnics with my siblings and my cousins in the 1930s. Our parents would allow us children to play hide-and-seek in the temple, run among the ruins and the statues. We played at giving them all kinds of names and imaginary personality traits—my favorite was "the Ruthless Hunter," a headless woman in marble with a spear resting against her right flank and the fingers of her left hand dug into the mane of a vanquished lion at her feet.

One of the high points of our daylong outings was a ritual dear to Uncle Ibrahim: a visit to a sprawling apiary run by a Sufi shepherd who always welcomed the two patriarchs very warmly, treating our uncle like a national hero. Together, the three men would reminisce about the proud nationalist tradition expressed by one single word among Benghazians who shared their belief: loyalty, the rallying cry that marked their enduring allegiance to Omar Mukhtar, the father of Libyan anti-Fascism, the Lion of the Desert who fought the good fight up to the day of his execution on September 16, 1931. Then they would go to a mud hut built by the Cyrenian shepherd, where he would sell them his finest honeys, including the rare and highly prized wild varieties harvested from the trees.

⁂

Loyalty. For us Khaldoons, this watchword was more than a political symbol. It was also a mode of belief and a day-to-day practice that helped our family remain faultlessly united in those days of deep unrest. The loyalty code instilled in us was all the more binding for being taught chiefly by example, with Mother and Father adhering to it strictly in their relationship. To take one example, loyalty played a major role in keeping our parents cohesive on the question of their daughters' upbringing, in helping them display flawless unity of purpose despite their deep differences regarding our schooling. It was not until my siblings and I were adults that we discovered Mother's divergence from Father on that crucial question. Mother grew up in a family with strongly held beliefs about equal education for girls. The Akrams, like many members of the Turkish aristocracy in Alexandria, staunchly adhered to the secularist tenets of Kemalism.

As for Father, his adherence to Sufism made him very progressive for a Libyan man of his generation, but his anti-Fascist politics were a major issue. Because Zaynab and I were officially kept in the dark about his political beliefs, we never suspected that his indignation over our enrollment in "Mussolini school" was deeply felt, and that he far preferred schooling at home for us, along with our weekly English lesson at the local book club with a Maltese restaurateur's wife. Much later in life, Mother told us she had come to suspect that Father secretly resented Zaynab and me for our Fascist education even as he presented a united front with her. But in the fevered urgency of those days, there was no room for suspicion—loyalty prevailed over everything else.

It was also out of loyalty that I resigned myself to accepting—abruptly, unconditionally—Father's dictum that Zaynab was the daughter with personality while I was the one with stamina.

I remember that particular moment in my life quite clearly: the winter of '36. It was a moment of waiting, in fear, in hope; of awed expectancy followed by a nameless pain that I had no choice but to keep to myself, not least because it was nameless. I was almost nine and had recently asked Mother if she would let me accompany Zaynab when she went around the quarter to invite the ladies in our neighborhood to her tea parties. Zaynab's rounds typically took place on Wednesday, our day off from school.

"I'll speak to your father about it," she had told me. "He is the one who decides these matters."

I learned of the verdict a few days later, when I returned from school. I remember approaching our house from the rear lane and through the back court, as usual. I opened the door to the patio and saw Auntie Mouna drawing water from the well at the opposite end by the stone wall that separated our house from the annex we rented out. She put down the bucket when she saw me, walked across the patio toward me, and took my hand, leading me to the fountain at the center. It was winter, and we never ran the fountain in the cold months, so we sat down on the rim of the basin, and I remember gasping and springing up as I felt the sting of the cold marble through my skirt. I wrapped my cape tightly around my thighs and sat back down.

She took hold of my hand again, sitting with me in silence for a moment. Looking up into her face, though, I was able to understand everything without any words being exchanged between us. Auntie Mouna's expression was as somber as the cold shadows of the walls around us. Her dilated pupils were like two disks of onyx in the center of those hazel eyes, and her radiant, ivory complexion had deepened to a dull shade of sallow gray. If it weren't for the colorful head wrap, our housekeeper might have been a woman in mourning during that instant of dejected stillness.

When she began to speak, her words were ponderous—maybe a bit shy, too—as if she were revealing something personal that she was loath to share with me.

"Madame Noor has asked me to tell you. Ahmad Basha gave her his decision this morning." Auntie Mouna was silent for a moment, still fixing those sad eyes on my face—her hand still folded around mine, her kohl smudging slightly. "I know you're disappointed," she resumed, "but your father knows your nature so well, *habibti*. He's right when he says the outdoor work is good for you. You have a lot of stamina, he said. That's the word he told Madame—*stamina*. Working with me in the courtyard, he said, helps you get rid of the extra energy, and I'm sure it does. I've seen it work wonders on you, Mariam. Also, Ahmad Basha says working outdoors helps you *sleep better* when you have those . . . helps . . . your sleeplessness."

I must have looked devastated sitting there under her scrutinizing gaze—my first bitter taste of rejection. She wanted to hold me in her arms, but I shook her off. "Leave me alone," I mumbled into her galabia as she tried to pull me closer. I, too, was beginning to tear up. I wanted this moment to be over.

Auntie Mouna had immediately read my mind.

"Come up with me to the laundry room," she said as she stood up. "Come on up to the rooftop. You can read to me from one of your books, or look out at the sea—it'll do you a world of good."

She went over to pick up the washboard by the kitchen door.

"Leave your satchel here, and let's go," she said, smiling with the washboard under her arm. "It's still plenty light out—you can see the new boats pulling into the harbor. You always like looking at the boats!"

My memory is not entirely clear as to what happened next on the outside stairs. I do recall, however, that Auntie Mouna was about two stairs ahead of me as we went up. At some point, she remembered the bucket she had left by the well.

"Good Lord! I forgot the bucket," she said, swinging around and slamming the corner of the board so hard into my mouth, I staggered sideways and fell back against the banister. The shock was extremely harsh, but it was also very sudden, and I was too confused to feel the pain at first. Then I looked up and saw the grimace of horror on our housekeeper's face, and all at once, her dread entered into my entire being—the realization that something had gone terribly wrong. I saw the blood dripping down onto my cape, resting intact for a few seconds on the black woolen fabric, like coral beads. I put my fingers to my mouth, and they came away stained.

The next thing I remember is the washboard clattering down the stairs and Auntie Mouna on her knees before me, her arms stretched out on either side of me—holding on to the railing, her face bent down so close to mine I could catch the scent of mastic gum on her breath, see the faint streaks of *miswak* across her immaculate ivory teeth.

"Please, for the love of God," she implored, "tell them you fell on the stairs! I'm done for if you say I hit you . . . finished. Awad will kill me!"

I cannot remember if it was the pain or the sight of Auntie Mouna's agony that triggered my tears, but I do know for certain that at some point, I just let myself sit back against the banister and cry—trapped between our housekeeper's outstretched arms as her face got closer and closer to mine, bigger and bigger, more and more twisted and tormented. Before long, I began to moan in pain and helplessness and sorrow—as if, through the supreme indignity of this final blow, I was now at last free to lament with the full force of my being the bleak sentence that had been handed down by the fountain.

"I beg you, please say you tripped and fell on the stairs, or Awad will kill me. God will never forgive me for this, I know, but please have mercy on your auntie Mouna! Say you tripped and fell on the stairs, in the name of God! I'll make it up to you, I swear. I'll make up for it a hundredfold."

I don't know how long I stayed like that—crying, moaning softly with my back against the iron banister, with her tearful, kohl-streaked face so close to mine. Eventually, though, I held on to a spindle and started to hoist myself up. Standing to her full height, Auntie Mouna stepped aside and let me stand up and head back to the house, trundling down the stairs alongside me, leaning over me with her arms still protectively held out on either side of my body, as if I might stumble at any moment and fall forward on my face. I was still crying, not so much with pain, perhaps, as with disconsolation—as if this hit had some dark, inscrutable connection with my father's fateful pronouncement.

Finally, she had to let me go ahead, walking slightly behind me, still damning herself, still imploring me to say that I had tripped.

Ali was the first to see me. He was in the kitchen, and I remember that he was eating a halva wrap: the sandwich we fondly called *aroussa* back then—"doll" or "beauty." He dropped it and ran out of the room, screaming for Mother.

"*Ya' Allah!*" Mother screamed as she saw me. "What happened to you?"

"I fell over and hit my mouth," I lied, turning around and looking up at Auntie Mouna for confirmation—the smart of my lip wound electric and jarring, like a toothache, the lower corner of my mouth smoldering. *This is the price I have to pay for telling lies*, I thought, and all at once, I realized that I was going to have to speak without my lips touching if I wanted to keep from hurting even more.

"I was going up to the laundry room with Auntie Mouna, and I fell facedown on the stairs."

I will never forget the look of gratitude on her face as the words came out of my torn mouth, clownishly aspirated and guttural. I lied for her sake, out of blind loyalty, and she was so moved that she began to cry again.

"I am deeply shaken, Madame. It was dreadful seeing my little Mariam hurting!"

"Let me see your mouth under the light," Mother said, her eyes still fixed on me with a frown, as if she had difficulty making sense of my story.

We stepped outside the kitchen door into the area we called the foyer. In our house, this was not an ordinary entrance hall but a nameless architectural hybrid placed in a median position between the forbidden space of the men's salon and the huge all-purpose room we called "the women's drawing room." That oddly named foyer gave no access to the outer perimeter of our house—a completely hermetic space accessible only through the doors of the three rooms abutting it: the kitchen and the two segregated drawing rooms. There was also the staircase that led up to our bedrooms, with a large crystal chandelier hanging over it—the light Mother had in mind. She switched it on and had me sit at the bottom of the stairs. She then asked me to tilt my head back, grasping my chin and pulling down my lower lip with her thumb.

"Ah naht a cah, ya nah!" I shouted.

"Hush up!" Mother whispered. "Your sister is sick upstairs. And now you. There'll be a bad bruise on your chin for a while, but your lip . . . It's nothing. You split your lower lip slightly. Nothing a strong girl like you can't handle. We're going to the infirmary at once. We'll get you stitched up."

I'm not a cow, you know! That was what I was trying to say, but with my excessive fear of any bilabial contact, my words came out as an incomprehensible jumble. "Ah naht a cah," I repeated.

"What?" Mother exclaimed. "You have to stop straining your wound till we get you stitched up, understand?"

Hearing those words from Mother, I just couldn't help it: the retort shot out of me with a force of sarcasm and levity that both scared and excited me. "Neh ahnd—it hah een saining ahl ahtanoon," I replied, deliberately exaggerating the distortion in my pronunciation. *Never mind—it has been straining all afternoon* was what I both said and didn't say, taking both solace and pleasure in the realization that I could now use my injury as a secret weapon— get away with telling her what had been on my mind since Auntie Mouna's dreadful revelation at the fountain.

Mother rolled her eyes. She ignored my words and took a step behind me. I turned around with a secret shiver of anticipation. The cubby-size alcove wedged between the staircase and the women's drawing room functioned like a miniature walk-in closet—it had a high shelf for our candlesticks and our stock of candles, along with a wall-mounted rack underneath it for the coats of the ladies who socialized with us. The shelf was also where her wallet was—a wristlet wallet of dark-green leather in which she kept some money for daily expenses. She reached up for it, opened it, pulled out a couple of slips and several bills. She took a look at the slips, counted the bills, and put everything into her purse, which could only mean that she was going to accompany me to the infirmary.

※

"You stay right here with my boy," Mother said to Auntie Mouna and Antar when we got to the infirmary—the one opposite Scuola Elementare e Media Giovanni Gentile, where my sister and I went.

Then the two of us stepped inside the building, and immediately, my oversensitive nerves and allergy-prone nose started reacting to the smell of formaldehyde with a violence that made me feel staggered and puny. We had barely walked into the hallway, and I was already overwhelmed by a dread for which I had no name.

"'lease, 'other," I pleaded. "I ah sick . . . I han't walk." And I actually began to bury my face between the flaps of her wrap coat, pulling them toward me in a futile attempt to conceal myself from the metallic reek and raw nakedness of this place—its glaringly lit, shockingly white-walled starkness.

"Come now, child." Mother stopped and argued with me gently. "If we don't take care of your wound now, your lip will be marked with an ugly scar—for the rest of your life. You have to be strong, my darling, and it'll be over in a few minutes. Believe me, *habibti*, it's going to be very quick."

I was still unresponsive, still holding on to her coat as to a curtain, trying to hide my face. That was when she decided to force me inside. Mother put her arms around my shoulders and steered me toward the small waiting room, which was empty and had an even stronger alcohol smell than the hallway.

"Look at me, child," Mother said as soon as we were seated. "Come now, look at me. You want this to be over, right?"

I was leaning sideways in my chair, still holding on to her coat, still sickened by the shock of the place. She cupped my head in her gloved hands and lifted it slowly but strongly until our gazes met—the emerald eyes looking down at me with more sadness than resolve in them; the oval countenance firmly framed by a silver-gray, slip-on head wrap, not a single wisp of her honey-blonde hair escaping it. It was the first time in my existence that I found myself studying my mother's appearance with a measure of detachment, and for all the emotionless frigidity of that moment and that space, I could not help but find some form of nameless solace in the sheer beauty of the woman who bore and reared me: the statuesque evenness of her alabaster face, the subtle blush of her cheeks, the wistful lift of her sandy eyebrows.

"You want this to be over soon?" she repeated, her tone urgent but not hard, her eyes still sad. "Am I right? Answer me now."

"Right, Mother," I said, instinctively realizing that it was in my best interest to tell her what she wanted to hear.

"All right, then. There's only one thing you need to do if you want the whole thing done quickly and without pain. As soon as they take you in and ask you to sit down, be sure to keep your eyes closed till they're finished. Promise me you'll do that, *habibti*, and everything will be all right. Promise?"

Once again, I had to tell Mother what she wanted to hear. I promised, and for a moment felt relieved and not so weak anymore.

Then an orderly stepped into the room, and I found myself flashing back to that feeling of frozen fear in the hallway. He was the same mysterious man I would notice every now and then outside the infirmary—a gaunt, chain-smoking, tobacco-skinned Sicilian who wore an outsize lab coat, a precarious comb-over, and bottle-bottom glasses that obscured his gaze and gave him a deceptively sinister air. Most of his body was completely indiscernible under that incongruous white coat.

When he saw the horror on my face, the orderly gave me a coffee- and tobacco-stained grin, which made me feel even more faint and agitated. He called out to one of the female nurses—an Egyptian name, to my relief.

"Rateeba!" he almost shouted.

"That's right, bring in someone really orderly—exactly what I need at this point."* I whispered the words in Mother's direction, as coolly and as articulately as possible, even though I was fully aware that my mouth was going to hurt.

Mother couldn't help it. She burst into half-suppressed laughter.

"You and your bizarre jokes!" she exclaimed, trying to sound dismissive and save face in front of the man.

The combination of the pleasure taken in that quip and the pain burning in my mouth made me feel heroic all of a sudden,

---

* In Arabic, the word *rateeba* refers both to a given name and to the female form of the adjective *orderly* or *tidy*.

almost elated. I suddenly realized that bizarre jokes or not, if I could raise a laugh in Mother in this place, I could certainly walk with Rateeba to the dreaded operating room and face my ordeal alone.

※

Back in the waiting room, Mother tipped Rateeba and inspected the stitches, holding my chin between her thumb and index finger, scrutinizing the nurse's craftsmanship with the same critical frown that would darken her face when she supervised our schoolwork at home.

"Thank you, Sit Rateeba. How is her wound now?" she asked, looking up at the nurse.

"Like it never happened!" Rateeba chimed in, jawing on a big lump of mastic gum as she spoke. She handed Mother a vial of iodine and a small box of cotton batting. "They're absorbable sutures—no need to come back. Just don't forget to disinfect it on a regular basis. And no more yawning in class for the next fortnight," she said to me, pinching my cheek with a mischievous smile—a jocular familiarity that Mother was in no mood to tolerate.

"My daughter is no yawner, take my word for it. Her trouble is actually allowing herself to sit back and take it easy every now and then. Goodbye, Nurse."

※

Out in Piazza del Municipio, I felt the full lash of the chill, damp wind and was all at once thrown back into that fateful moment at the fountain—feeling cut off and forlorn in the raw air. We were walking toward the horse-drawn streetcar, and my somber thoughts must have infected Ali, who trailed behind the four of us with a listless, dejected air. Four mighty draft horses had just been hitched to the coach while the outgoing ones stood stone-still by the curb in their blankets, their heads lowered against the damp wind. Mother urged us all to get on the streetcar, but my brother stood motionless beside the idle horses, staring into space and frowning, absently grinding his heel into a gap between the cobblestones.

We all rushed to his side. "What is it, son?" Mother inquired, bending over him with a tender solicitude she never showed me. All eyes were on Ali now. We stood within arm's reach of the resting horses, and the air was rife with their body heat, the sweet scent of their sweat.

"Stupid stairs!" he blurted out, still sullen and unmoving, struggling to suppress his tears and put up a tough front. "Ruined my sister's mouth like . . . like . . . a busted firecracker!" His voice was shaky and tearful. The sight of me bleeding had deeply unsettled him from the start, but seeing me now with the stitches was more than he could bear. Ali was born in early June and hadn't turned thirteen yet, but he had always seen himself as my older brother and felt deeply protective of me. He was on the verge of tears when he uttered those words, and yet his phrasing was so colorful that none of us women could help ourselves. We all just burst out laughing at his interjection—the stunningly pertinent image of how useless a firecracker could appear once it was "busted." And in the days that followed, his words proved utterly apt: that sutured lip rendered my whole mouth fragile and unreliable, no matter how sparingly or carefully I tried to use it.

"Oh, brother," I told him, "you do so cherish me, don't you?"

"Very much!" he replied. His voice shook with heartbreaking emotion.

"Come now," Mother said, getting emotional herself. "Tomorrow this little accident will be nothing more than a bad memory, my son. Come, let's treat ourselves to some Perugina from Pasticceria Tre Marie. I hear there's nothing better than chocolate to heal *anything*, especially an injured lip, no matter how busted it is."

※

The horsecar, which was designed to resemble an American "white bus" from the 1920s, was already quite full when we boarded. We had to sit toward the back in the wooden-seat section. The driver kept taking additional passengers, though, probably more than the vehicle could carry safely. By the time we rolled out of Piazza del Municipio, the windows had begun to fog up, and the air inside the packed carriage became dense, humid, and charged with the rank redolence of damp wool and stale tobacco. Auntie Mouna sat in the aisle seat beside me. I swiveled my torso to the right, sliding down and nestling my head in the crook of her arm—the feltlike softness of her Berber burnoose. I reckoned that if I sat lower and narrowed my field of vision to the wedge of space between her cloaked body and the wooden window frame to my right, I might be able to shut out the stifling presence of the passengers crowded around me, let my gaze wander out to the street.

By now the windowpane had turned into an unevenly translucent glass plate misted over with a grainy, discontinuous film of vapor that warped and diffused the colors of the ordinary street scenes blurring by as we rattled down Via Briccola—nebulous, shifting patterns of clustered dots and drops like the frenzied, unfinished work of an impatient spray painter. The driver stopped at the main post office, and I caught myself playing a game: narrowing my eyes and tilting my head slightly, visualizing the wide neoclassical building at the end of the long, slate-cobbled alley as one of the messy watercolors I would paint with Mother's awkward help. In my moment of fantasy, the building metamorphosed into the softly contoured picture of a rain-eroded sandcastle, with its twin turrets worn down to gritty nubs. The alley became a path made with licorice squares; the palmetto-, agave-, and oleander-studded lawn on either side of the path a foggy jungle growth of scratches and smears in overlapping shades of green and brown and pink.

Mother shared the seat ahead of us with Ali. I sat up when she turned around to speak to Auntie Mouna, suddenly feeling

I needed to find reassurance in that alabaster face, glowing with radiance above the metal frame of the shabby seat—a sad, sentimental urge to be alone with her in our house, to bury my face in the scented shadows of her coat, the protective embrace of her arms.

But in that moment, she was all business again—her eyes remote and dark and hard as I sat and looked up at her with all my emptiness and nameless longing. She held out a rectangular white envelope through the loop of the metal headrest. "I want you to go to Dar Toota," she said to Auntie Mouna, "and hand the letter back to Monsieur Fribourg's secretary. Tell her Ahmad Basha has read it and has charged you to inform the boss that there is no need for a letter of recommendation—Monsieur Fribourg's word is all he needs in terms of a guarantee. We will vacate the annex as soon as he, Mr. Fribourg, tells us the tenants are ready to move in. I also want you to go to Nikiforakis. Ahmad Basha's travel-permit photos are ready. Here's the receipt. We'll wait for you around Piazza Cagni."

The streetcar stopped at Market Square. Auntie Mouna stood up and Antar sat down in her place. I slid off the wooden seat and inched over to the window, resting my right forearm on its lower frame. I wiped away the condensation with the heel of my left hand; the full-size orange trees that marked off the red-brick court of our outdoor market stood as radiant as ever in their wooden planter boxes. Their immaculate leaves were treated with leaf shine, as usual, and the navel oranges glowed like lanterns in the blue-green foliage. Beyond those neatly spaced planters, there was the customary motley scene of our market: dazzling arrays of roses and flowers in florists' stands and the most amazing fruits and vegetables artfully arranged in the stalls and on the carts, their colors glistening, beckoning in the distance like the hypnotic hues of exotic porcelain novelties.

I saw Auntie Mouna's dark-cloaked form spring off the running board and merge into the crowd of market shoppers—the only burnoosed woman on the sidewalk, her perfect Nefertitian face glowing like ivory inside the black hood. The horsecar pulled out and I kept following Auntie Mouna with my eyes, observing our housekeeper work her way through the throng toward the Moorish arcade that housed the mall known among Benghazians by the rather exotic name of "the Indian Bazaar," a cluster of shops that contrasted dramatically with Suq al Dhalaam—their echoes of faraway mythical lands and dreamy experiences.

Monsieur Fribourg's establishment, Dar Toota, or Mulberry's, was the first and most prominent shop in the Indian Bazaar. In fact, it was considered the finest fancy-goods store in our city. Its owner—we knew him only as Monsieur Fribourg—was a French Jewish gentleman whose parents had migrated to Tunisia when he was very young. He spoke French, Italian, and Judeo-Tunisian Arabic. The shop was named after his daughter, Deborah, who was my classmate and went by the nickname Toota. Father conducted all his local banking affairs with Monsieur Fribourg, shunning "Mussolini's banks" altogether. In those days, all business transactions in Benghazi involved cash payments, and Father, like any other important businessman in town, had to have adequate liquidity resources at all times. The gentleman from France made that possible in a speedy, efficient manner and at rates that were more competitive than those charged by the local banks.

Auntie Mouna went through the portico on the market side of the bazaar and into a side door. The horsecar proceeded down the roofed section of Via Briccola, past Dar Toota's breathtaking main entrance—the hand-carved arabesques of its Moroccan archway, the amber glow of its twin copper-encased Andalusian lamps hanging over the door from their iron chains. Soon, we would enter Via Torino—moments away from the splendors of Piazza Cagni.

✻

We got off at Palazzo Prosdocimo, a monumental Art Deco department store on the piazza. We were not going into any of the shops, so Mother and I crossed over to the roundabout in the middle of the square—the only shelter from the dust kicked up by passing traffic. There was not much of either, but my nasal symptoms were definitely a matter of concern to Mother, who did not want me itching and sneezing and complaining about how unbearable the very idea of dust was. Those were the mid-thirties, and Piazza Cagni had not yet been paved—plain red Benghazi dirt with fine and volatile dust that was stirred up by the slightest breeze, finding its way into your nose, settling on your clothes and on your face.

Our convenient haven in the middle of the street junction was a monumental disc of concrete circling a low, turf-covered mound with a majestic Sicilian fir at its center. Mother and I headed straight for that inner island of grass and waited for Ali and Antar, who had been dispatched to buy the chocolates from Pasticceria Tre Marie, opposite Prosdocimo. There was only a trickle of traffic around us—the occasional truck or car, a few buggies and bicycles coming and going—but somehow, we both knew that in my present mood, I needed to feel protected, and the best way for me to find protection, we tacitly agreed, was to wait on that impeccably groomed lawn. And I did indeed feel safe and sheltered standing in the shadow of the tree, my spirits unexpectedly lifting even as the sky had shifted. We had not been there more than a few minutes when the sun broke out from behind the clouds, just as it began to slip below the roofline of Palazzo Prosdocimo. The metamorphic, amber glow of that lowering sun had suddenly transmogrified the entire east side of the square, muted its daunting architectural grandeur into a chiaroscuro scene of enchantment: our Art Deco Municipal Theater—the marmoreal monumentalism of its ice-white rectangular planes and its blind arcade of stilted arches shifting to a grisaille of dark ginger root and burnt umber; the imposing sandstone facade of the Military Association—pilasters receding into the shadows like half-melted wax tablets; the avenue of slender palm trees along Viale della Stazione stretching out to the eastern horizon in soft, paper-cut silhouettes. All of it already fading as fast as a chimera, thanks to the treacherous transience of our desert afterglow.

⁎

I do not remember at what precise moment the Tuareg woman spotted us, but I certainly recall her husband's voice, and how Mother and I turned around at the eerie, muffled sound of it.

"Markunda!" he yelled and went on shouting at her in Berber.

"Stay right there—I won't be long!" she shouted back in a strange, Maghrebi Arabic dialect—not from around these parts, and not from east of here, either. Probably Algeria.

We stood firmly within the protective perimeter of our green island, staring at them in amazement. The man was leading two gigantic camels: the one he held in rein was burden-free and elegantly saddled, whereas the other looked overloaded and had its rope halter tied to the backrest of the lead animal's seat. It appeared that those monumental ships of the desert had crossed over from the Prosdocimo edge of the square, just like us, and their human leader was now hovering miserably around Mother and me, protesting as his wife commenced to approach us. She had already stepped onto the concrete ring of the roundabout, leaving her husband decidedly behind her, as if he were a burden or an embarrassment. And so, he came to a halt just a few steps from the circular structure, with his face all but invisible within the folds of his litham. The hood of his burnoose was pulled down low, which made his voice sound remote and cavernous.

"Come back here, woman!" he moaned, in an Arabic dialect this time, even as a Fiat truck came roaring around in a cloud of dust, nearly grazing the second beast's rump. The driver was in no rush to move on, though. Hitting the brakes unnecessarily, well after he had cleared that poor underdog camel, he leaned on his horn and out of the window, taking his time to hurl an elaborate insult at the stranded stranger.

While a visibly serene Markunda walked on toward us, unperturbed by the Italian truck driver's arbitrary display of machismo—a broad smile on her face, which did not betray any hint of the strain of desert travel, her immaculate teeth flashing like chalk between freshly painted dark-purple lips. She wore the traditional indigo turban deliberately loose to show off her pleasing countenance, her raven hair, and the marvelous Tuareg-cross earrings she wore. The mysterious woman had now crossed all the way over to our grassy little haven and was standing right before us. Markunda's eyes were the first thing I noticed as I studied her face: their aquamarine luminescence contrasted strangely with the copper glow of her flushed cheeks, and the strangeness was ineffably compelling, haunting beyond words. Suddenly, all of this seemed so beautifully unreal: the otherworldly garb and ravishingly rakish demeanor of this strange woman who had materialized from nothingness, just like our chance intimation of spring in the dead of winter. There were now three of us, as Mother and I clung to the last rays of the sun, sharing our haven of lush lawn and crisp, fir-scented air with Markunda—her endless eyes and irresistible smile, her bizarre offer to talk to me about what she called the "path of my destiny."

"My husband and I were just passing through here," she said. "We could have kept going, but I saw you were hurt, and I knew I had to stop and talk to you about the path of your destiny. Fate has made our paths cross—it has put me in your way so that I can help you understand the meaning of what happened to you today."

She had now switched to standard Arabic—awkwardly eloquent and imperfect but fully understandable, notwithstanding the staccato cadence of her Algerian accent. We stood facing east, and the twilight sky was like the mottled hollow of a clay oven, the still palms like raven feathers on charred sticks.

"Look," she said, and waved her hand, encompassing the horizon, "the wind has quieted, and the sun—even the sun—is giving you a sign. It's telling you how many beautiful things life has in store for you—in spite of the injury and all the grief. Listen, I am a seer, and I can help you with my powers. Let me tell you what I see, and then I'll give you something that you will keep with you at all times. It will protect you day and night."

Mother was suspicious and dismissive. "My good woman," she interjected, "we're just like you, strange as it may seem. Passing through. No time for fate and signs and all that. Just get back to your husband, and leave my daughter alone. Keep to *your* path. And make sure you always introduce yourself as a fortune-teller—it'll *sell* better."

I very much wanted Markunda to read my fortune, though, and I wished the woman would stand fast. But Ali and Antar had emerged from the pastry shop and put a stop to my wishful wonderings. They stood under the marquee, laughing and trying to stuff their mouths with what looked like chunks of pinkish pastry, tossing back their heads with every bite so that they wouldn't miss a single crumb of whatever it was they were eating—a patently ineffective approach, judging from the crumb scatterings on the breasts of their coats. Ali was laughing so hard, he staggered backward against the marquee post, still tilting back his head in a vain attempt to keep the crumbs from landing on his coat.

"*Ya' Allah*, he's going to choke right before my eyes. As if I haven't had enough turmoil for today!"

"Don't you worry, Madame. I'll get them!" Auntie Mouna was just about to join us, but instead, she hopped off the roundabout and headed straight across the junction toward the marquee under which my brother and her son stood, unaware of being observed, trying to brush off all evidence of their surreptitious purchase and doing a miserable job of it.

Meanwhile, the lead camel, having somehow managed to edge its way onto the roundabout behind its master's back, began to put its size and the astonishing length of its neck to excellent use. With its hind legs half-folded and its forelegs lowered onto the concrete surface, it bent down its head, stretched its neck as far out as it could, and commenced to sample the lawn on which we stood—raising its head critically after the first few bites, chewing the grass of our finest roundabout even as its follower stayed put on the other side, looking as forlorn and left out as the scorned husband.

Inevitably, the Tuareg man felt a tug on the reins and turned around. Seeing what was happening, he had no choice but to step onto the concrete ring and rush toward the beast, trying to dissuade it, cursing his fate in Maghrebi Arabic, mumbling something about "the Sudanese watchman"—an Eritrean carabiniere standing guard by his candy-striped sentry box outside the Military Association building.

"Give them some carob," Markunda ordered her husband. "That'll keep them from getting into trouble with the soldier. Chomping on the Italians' fancy grass . . . nobody is going to like that here—certainly not *him* over there!"

"*Their* grass!" Mother shouted. But before she could launch into a political lecture on Libya being *our* country and everything in it being *ours*, the carabiniere came striding across the junction, rifle ominously unslung, and stood squarely facing the terrified Tuareg. Outside the pastry shop, the rest of our party stood on the edge of the sidewalk, petrified with fear and surprise, eyes riveted on the surreal scene.

The Eritrean carabiniere addressed his vis-à-vis in awkward, strongly guttural Hijazi Arabic, which made the words tumbling out of his mouth even more threatening and peremptory: "This camel stays away from the lawn once and for all. That, or he will be shot."

But then Markunda, who had already anticipated the confrontation without us even noticing, had managed to bring forth two feed bags from the loaded camel, holding them up with a broad smile and a prestidigitator's panache. Not only was she unfazed by the brutal show of force, but she was clearly having her fun.

"*Kharroobbo, signore!*" she exclaimed in awful Italian. "*Kharroobbo, per favore. Bono camele, per favore! Tutto bene!*"

"*Carrubo*," he corrected her with an expression of amazement and immitigable disgust on his face, failing to acknowledge the humor in the seer's deliberate shift from Arabic to Italian.

Her satiric gesture was not lost on Mother, though. As soon as the officer was gone, she turned to face Markunda with a smile.

The my-good-woman condescension of a moment before had given way to solidarity—also gone was the outrage at the two boys' pastry shenanigans.

Mother said, "I was going to dismiss you out of hand just then, but seeing how this lout treated you and the rest of us, camels included, I will stand my ground right here and we will take our time and have you read my daughter's fortune. We will eat the chocolate right here, just to spite that no-good, boorish occupier."

"Amen to that!" Markunda exclaimed.

※

The reading did not last more than ten or fifteen minutes, and yet Markunda was able to put her finger on some of the most crucial things my inner world revolved around: the inexplicable sensitivities; the middle-of-the-night onslaughts of unruly ideas and unrelenting mental energy; the sudden clouds of anxiety and underachievement guilt. I remember her examining me with those uncanny eyes in all their mesmerizing, unearthly beauty. Markunda punctuated her prophecy with beautifully choreographed, serpentine hand movements that made the silver bangles on her left wrist tinkle like glass chimes. My rare gifts, she said, would come with great challenges and fears, but by and by, I was bound to triumph over all those hurdles, going on to do things no girl had ever done before.

"You wake up in the middle of the night, Mariam," she said. "Many a night. Full of trepidation and longing. You see very far and hope and pray for all the things you see. Despite your unusual height and physical strength, the longings in your heart are far greater than the power of your body, child. But your body will catch up, and then you will do the things you are destined to do—deeds the world will marvel to behold. You will travel far, and the work of your hands will surpass all human imaginings."

Markunda suddenly fell silent, lifted up her right hand, and contemplated it for the briefest second. She then worked a luminous rosary off her wrist and let it slide down into the hollow of her upturned palm, its beads throbbing with an opalescent glow.

"Mariam," she declared as she held out the gift to me, "with this blessed rosary by your bedside, you need never fear waking in the middle of the night. Reach for it every time your heart wakes in the cold darkness, and you will find it to be comforting and reliable. Hold it in your right palm, and keep gazing at it in the dark as you recite these words that I am about to give you."

I took her gift with my right hand.

The seer glanced to her left, then her right. Seeing that there were no adult males around except for her husband, she pulled down her turban and, reaching behind her head, lifted up a dark-brown deerskin pouch she was wearing on a leather string around her neck. Unlacing the drawstring of the pouch, she pulled out a wafer-thin, oddly luminescent, yellowish thing that looked like a jagged shard of honeycomb or shale. She kept the object on the flat of her right palm and held it out for me to see. It was an age-old piece of thick paper inscribed with very fine Kufic script written in carbon ink and arranged in the shape of a labyrinthine seal.

"This is the greatest safeguard of all." She sighed, perhaps with a hint of regret. "The Verse of the Throne. During the day, you will wear it on your breast like a shield. It's from my grandmother, and now it's yours. Keep it in its pouch at all times. It will protect you day and night."

She put her hand on my head and recited: *"Allah! There is no deity but Him, the Alive, the Eternal. Neither slumber nor sleep overtaketh Him. Unto Him belongeth whatsoever is in the heavens and whatsoever is in the earth. Who could intercede in His presence without His permission? He knoweth that which is in front of them and that which is behind them, while they encompass nothing of His knowledge except what He wills. His throne includeth the heavens and the earth, and He is never weary of preserving them. He is the Sublime, the Tremendous."*

※

Night had all but descended—it was time to go. Mother had paid Markunda, and the seer and her husband had vanished from our life as swiftly and chimerically as they had entered it. The pouch with the blessed Koranic verse dangled from my neck, and the magical rosary was in my coat pocket. We headed for the tall, reddish lantern that marked the horsecar stop as the facade of Prosdocimo became ablaze, with its multicolored web of light strings winking on and off—a luminescent gingerbread house with its amber-glow display windows like stage sets just before curtain-up.

"Listen," I whispered to Ali as we entered the horsecar, "what were you eating back there outside the pastry shop?"

"Oh, something very special."

"Tell me—what was it?"

"It's made with a special berry."

"Strawberry, of course."

"No, stupid. If it was strawberry, I would have told you. It's a special berry from *Europe*, and *you* have never eaten it."

"You were eating pastry with a special berry?"

"It's not a pastry, simpleton. It's a sort of puffy candy. *Meerang*—that's what they call it. It's French."

"What?"

I have never ceased to wonder: Why was it so important for me to accompany my sister on her Wednesday rounds? Why did I choose to immure myself in silence—never pleading with Mother, never protesting?

Loyalty, again, along with the feeling, deeply seated in our collective imagination, that we all lived in hard and trying times—cruel times of pervasive precariousness that were relentlessly testing our strength and endurance, both as individuals and as a family; times that were always threatening to destroy our livelihood, nullify our prosperity. And so, with that awareness hanging over our heads like a sinister cloud, we accepted as a matter of course that we should never take our wealth for granted, finding assurance and order in the work structure set up by our father—the tasks that were essential for our survival as an economic entity and that were somehow made inseparable from our existential stability as a family unit.

In the early thirties, sales volume at the Whale was not solely dependent on the foreign goods that came in through the port of Benghazi—in fact, that segment of our business didn't carry a wide profit margin. The products my father and brothers brought into Libya from their grueling trade trips to Egypt and Sudan were far more profitable: cross-border imports that allowed the company to maintain its competitive edge, along with its capacity to offer a wide variety of the low-profit-margin imports we carried in stock at the wholesale store and in Uncle Ibrahim's spice and herb shop.

In those days, Libya's economy was hurting from the Great Depression, and our men had to adopt increasingly aggressive business strategies. Several times a year, the three Khaldoon men would lead a caravan of six or eight trucks on a trek, during which they took the most arcane, roundabout itineraries, making the most out-of-the-way stops en route to Alexandria—an obscure network of back roads and rural communities in the desert that only their Tuareg guide knew. They were recognizable in every oasis, every town, and every hamlet along the way, never failing to stop in and do business with the locals, no matter how small their population. But those trips were not risk-free, even in the early thirties. The men who crewed on the caravan had to be more than astute traveling salesmen. They were natural risk-takers, willing to accept the fact that carrying pistols and rifles and eventually using them against urban robbers and Bedouin bandit gangs was a normal part of their job. An Italian army connection in Benghazi took care of all permits and travel documents. In Alexandria, it was Uncle Kareem who handled the paperwork and kept the Egyptian and Sudanese officials happy.

Among the products that my father and my two brothers brought in from Egypt and Sudan, gold, jewelry, textiles, makeup, and foundation garments were the goods with the highest profit margins. Every member of our household was expected to perform at least one important task that revolved around those imports. Mother and Zaynab were to put together tea parties in the women's drawing room for the prominent ladies of Benghazi and its environs, presenting the wedding jewelry, dowry gold coins, accessories, perfumes, and makeup our men imported. During those precious klatches—effectively, advertising showcases—we served coffee, tea, and Levantine ice creams and pastries catered by Auntie Fatima, the Algerian wife of our local Lebanese pastry chef and Mother's protégé. We also served Italian chocolates and candies that Ali would fetch from Pasticceria Tre Marie.

As for me, my main task consisted in working with Auntie Mouna and Antar during those Wednesdays that were so crucial to the company's success. Wednesday was known among us women as "fabric day"—an exceptional and noisy happening in our house—a day during which, except for Antar's participation, the front yard metamorphosed into an exclusively female territory. This was a frenzied working space where the textiles that were brought in from Egypt would go through the final stage of processing before delivery to Benghazi's retailers. The imported fabrics came tied in bundles of neatly folded fat quarters, a typical bundle containing ten squares of material, eighteen by twenty-two inches each. Every time the returning caravan rolled into Benghazi, those bundles were immediately taken to the Moroccan tannery on Sidi Salem Alley, across from our home. There, they were dyed, fixated, and processed in special vats exclusively reserved for the transformation of our fabrics. Pressing each individual square of fabric was the last stage in the process, and it was done in our front courtyard by a half dozen professional ironers under the supervision of Auntie Mouna and me.

Preparations for that day's work started early in the morning. After the men left for work, Auntie Mouna and Antar would begin by putting out cloth-covered trestle tables on the cobbled end of the men's courtyard, between the gate and the outer door of the men's salon. Then our housekeeper would light the brazier for the ironers, who would show up later with their flat irons. On fabric day, my job consisted in observing the court and liaising between Mother and the workers. I was also in charge of supervising Antar as he conveyed the material from the Sidi Salem tannery to the ironers. Equipped with a wheelbarrow, we would both go out through the men's gate to the tannery, where he would load up some of the processed fabric, wheel it back to our house, and pile it in a huge box next to the trestle tables. The ironers would then proceed to press the material, fold it, and stack it in perfectly tied ten-square bundles. Considering the large quantity of fabric imported by our men, working with the ironers on any given Wednesday involved a lot of shuttling back and forth between our house and the Moroccan tannery. The Wednesday workers were paid by Mother in person, and Auntie Mouna took care of all their needs, which included a free lunch and two tea breaks with candy and pastries from the Lebanese pastry store. The lunch was brought in from the next-door European-style restaurant, which was owned and managed by a Maltese chef. The ironers were always very jovial when they ate, making jokes about the food being "male cooking."

※

Looking back on those Wednesdays and their unspoken implications, I tend to think they ultimately allowed us to imagine that we were happy in spite of everything; safe in our shared conviction that if we were *feeling* happy, it was because we were united under a compact of unfailing family loyalty protecting us against the forces of enmity and unpatriotic betrayal raging around us.

Then, all of a sudden, in 1937, Mussolini—the real flesh-and-blood man—came along, and everything about that compact changed, or so the story went, the secret, mythical story told by Mother within our family. In the tale, our father's destiny was sealed when the Fascist tyrant came into town, as if the entire fabric of his existence had come undone through the fated force of that one single day. In fact, hatred of the Fascists and a certain powerless rage against their governor-general in Tripoli had been festering within our father since the twenties—years during which he and Uncle Ibrahim were secretly involved in an increasingly brutalized Resistance while still maintaining local political influence. Even as he mounted wave after wave of police and military brutality, the governor-general of Libya began studying the possibility of neutralizing that influence through a more subtle political strategy.

Starting in the early thirties, the Fascist ruler, who was well aware that the Mahdi and Khaldoon families were the most powerful funders of the Resistance, commenced to lure a few regional Bedouin chieftains with promises of prestige and extended powers for them, prosperity for the Benghazians as a whole, and even a measure of political autonomy for the region. The gambit worked with devastating efficiency. Through long-distance political maneuvering from Tripoli, the governor-general managed to provoke a ruthless feeding frenzy among local tribal and community leaders, resulting in a further weakening of the Resistance in our city and the ouster of Uncle Ibrahim from his position as unofficial mayor of Benghazi.

This reversal was a terrible blow to both our families. Although Uncle Ibrahim never lost his prestige and epic stature among Benghazians and Father's image as a prominent community leader remained intact, the two men had become, in political terms, purely symbolic figures. Even so, the terribly adverse political circumstances never quite managed to squelch their revolutionary ardor. Both uncle and nephew remained faithful to the tradition of Omar Mukhtar well into the thirties, when the political winds had definitively changed. Steadfastly, quixotically, both men also remained staunch financial supporters of the Resistance—as much out of rage and injured pride as out of a sense of obligation to the memory of the Lion of the Desert. They never reneged on their patriotic commitment to the hero's anti-Fascist creed, living in hopeful expectation of the end of their struggles, dreaming of the day when Libya would rid itself of "Mussolini's gang," as the Fascists were called in their circle.

Patriotic commitment or no, however, history was decidedly not on the two men's side in the unsettled political climate of the thirties. By the time Mussolini rode into town to promote his new vision for Libya, the preparatory groundwork had already been laid by the so-called Bedouin upstarts, and that was what hurt our father's pride most. Through the wholehearted support of a minority of shamelessly opportunistic natives, Libya was well on its way to becoming the Fourth Shore of Italy; the Gioventù Araba del Littorio had been founded, effectively making a number of young Benghazian nobodies members of the Fascist Party; and in school, we were now being indoctrinated with the utopian illusion of us becoming "special Italian citizens" in the very near future.

So, when all is said and done, when all the chaotic experiences of that period are put into perspective, the mythical notion that it was the visit of the monstrous Duce that broke our father's heart does not seem to hold up under objective scrutiny. It was all those years of successive defeats and brazen betrayals that destroyed his faith in humankind, creating a sustained buildup of bleak negativity that kept seething in his sensitive heart. That fateful day in the spring of 1937 was, at most, a trigger event that sent him tumbling into the depths of depression.

Still, the aura of a family myth has a comforting appeal that is hard to resist, especially during childhood and adolescence, because, ultimately, Mother's story was precisely that for her children: a therapeutically pacifying myth that allowed us to see our father's death two years after the dictator's visit in soothingly simple terms—as the tragic but heroic outcome of a clear-cut division between the forces of good and the forces of evil, between a happy world before the Duce's visit and a gloomy one after it. In short, our family myth of Mussolini allowed us to infuse the nightmare of the times with a measure of sense and congruity; it made it possible for us to abate the baffling shock of history's untimely intrusion into our father's life. The earth-shattering moment narrated to us by Uncle Ibrahim: a good man collapsed on a bag of Ethiopian coffee, gone beyond recall in one of the dark, dank chambers of the Whale, his fez fallen to the dirt floor.

⁂

The Duce's visit.

It was first brought into my young and precocious consciousness through our teachers' hyperbolic accounts at Scuola Elementare e Media Giovanni Gentile. Early on in the winter term, we were informed that the event was slated for the spring of 1937. Even so, we ended up spending most of the term learning about it and preparing for it, with the rhetoric of our teachers growing more intense as the fateful date approached. On the eve of the big day, during our first morning class, the history and geography teacher, Signorina Cordini, announced to us playfully but emotionally that the time had come for her to "reveal" some of the details of the visit. She told us that Mussolini's motorcade was going to parade through our city early tomorrow morning, through Via Balbia, the newly inaugurated military highway. After a brief inspection of the Mussolini Promenade, the Duce would be presented with an Arabian charger in a private ceremony led by a group of regional chieftains. That welcome gift from the "Cyrenian sages," as she called them, was among the more colorful visit-related facts we learned from Signorina Cordini, who inflicted on us an impassioned relation of the meeting's historic significance.

During tomorrow's service, we were told, the Duce would show our regional chieftains the ceremonial "Sword of Islam" that he had received in Tripoli, thereby requesting to assume his title as Protector of Islam in Benghazi, too. After the chieftains' endorsement, he would ride into town on his Arabian stallion, a benevolent guardian of the city and its Islamic heritage and traditions. Finally, our teacher concluded with "the most exhilarating revelation of all," proudly informing us that there was a rally scheduled for tomorrow morning in Piazza del Municipio, and we would all be attending—as spectators only, however, because we were an all-Libyan school. There was even a small viewing stand by the mosque set up especially for Scuola Elementare e Media Giovanni Gentile!

We spent the remainder of that school day rehearsing their Fascist songs and slogans and doing drill exercises in Italian history and geography—reciting ceaselessly, collectively, their hollow dates and phrases and places, their ghostly political liturgy on the advent of Fascism and its liberating role in Italy and Libya alike. Shortly before dismissal, our teachers asked us to file quietly out of the classrooms and assemble in the schoolyard, where our principal, Signora Taramelli, spoke to us from a raised platform about something that left us all dumbfounded: the Duce's visit to our school tomorrow after the rally. It was going to be not only a very special day for Benghazi, she proclaimed, but also a very, very special day for Scuola Elementare e Media Giovanni Gentile. From our outstanding institution, two exceptional pupils had been chosen to welcome the Duce here, in this recess yard, in the name of the entire school. I heard her mention my sister's name and mine; then she went on to provide additional details about tomorrow's schedule of activities and the meeting place where we were to wait for our teachers before heading out to Piazza del Municipio.

When our principal was done addressing us, she stepped off the platform and walked up to my sister, telling her to remain on the school grounds; our fellow pupils, who had begun to disband, were still reeling in disbelief, chattering excitedly about tomorrow. Signora Taramelli was an imposingly tall, athletic woman in her early thirties who always wore her silky, blue-black hair in a short, inverted bob with straight, pointy side bangs. When she addressed us pupils, her attitude was usually rather respectful, almost warm, but there was a decidedly daunting quality in the unflinching placidity, the unruffled depth of those steel-blue eyes. That and the Celtic toughness of her high cheekbones and angular jawline gave her an appearance of severity that probably belied a tender disposition. In preparation for tomorrow, she wore a uniform—the white shirt, black tie, black jacket, and black skirt of the Milizia Volontaria per la Sicurezza Nazionale, or MVSN. Her head was topped with a too-large black garrison cap emblazoned with the Italian Fighting Bands symbol and the gold Fascist eagle. Untypically, she addressed us in a machine-gun-like, staccato tone, and we both kept staring in stupefaction at her muscular self so suddenly and outlandishly metamorphosed into a soldier, barking out orders like an automaton. The ravishingly soft hair of our principal, ordinarily one of her most striking features, was lost in the stark, lusterless blackness of the martial cap, which, besides its glaringly unnatural and unbecoming appearance, seemed so uncanny and contrived—as if it were something she had borrowed from a man in a rash, hapless attempt to hide some deficiency in her person.

"You mind your teachers tomorrow morning," she snapped. "Mariam will mind Signorina Cordini. Zaynab will stay near Signora Cabrini. They will tell you what to do. Listen carefully, and do not deviate from their instructions. Everything will work out fine. It's going to be a glorious day for our city *and* for our school."

Our teachers stood at attention behind her, all of them looking tense and somewhat angry, though they were probably just worn out and horrifically nervous.

On our way back home with Antar, I talked to my sister about the big day.

"Why was Signora Taramelli so upset when she told us to mind the teachers?" I asked.

"She wasn't upset," Zaynab replied impatiently. "It's the overbite—sometimes it makes her upper teeth clamp down on her lower lip as if she's mad. She's very nice, though; don't worry."

"I'm not worried!" I said.

※

The next morning, we sat down to breakfast as usual, which was always just the two of us girls and Antar; our men always breakfasted shortly after Morning Prayer, leaving for the wholesale store as soon as they had finished their meal. Antar was in charge of escorting us to school and back. He had his father's build and, at thirteen, was already as tall as a man and almost as strong. He ate like a man, too, and we enjoyed letting him help us finish our food, slipping some of it onto his plate and watching him gobble up the evidence in a few wolfish bites. We had Egyptian breakfast every morning, and so for our escort, the fare wasn't at all different from what his mother served in their home: *mudammas*, or fava beans; hard-boiled eggs; Egyptian falafel—we called them *tamiya*—and Domiati cheese served on a plate with olives and a drizzle of olive oil.

Today, Zaynab and I had managed to start our morning in quiet indifference, trying to be oblivious to yesterday's shrill conversation with Mother, trying to be oblivious to the much-ballyhooed event. We stared sleepily into our plates and half ate our food, and for a moment, our breakfast went on being just another ordinary, sluggish school-day ritual. Until Mother finally broke her silence.

She said, "Your father didn't sleep a wink last night, you know that? He was still in his work clothes, poor man, when he made ablution for the Dawn Prayer. I haven't seen him this upset since the day Uncle Ibrahim was ousted! He told me you two had been chosen on purpose. They did it to spite and mock him—the Judicial Authority. Those thugs plotted it with the MVSN. That's what your father said. May Benghazi be his last destination—this heartless, murderous butcher!"

She motioned Auntie Mouna to bring our school uniforms and coats.

"Which way will you be going?" she snapped as we stood up.

The question wasn't banal—a deliberate, terrible reminder of our conversation yesterday evening and Mother's burst of temper when we had told her about the uncustomary meeting place where we were to wait for our teachers.

"Mother, really, it's no big deal," Zaynab said, speaking for both of us. "I know where we're going from the moment we step out of the women's gate. All we have to do is take a right at the end of Sabir Alley and head toward Marsa Street instead of the usual route. Then we'll cross *our* street, Mahdi, and head straight for the fish market. That's it. Ali showed us the spot yesterday. On our way to the piazza, we'll be walking right by our house and up Sidi Salem, past Uncle Ibrahim's shop. It's all very simple, Mother. I know the way perfectly—from the women's gate to the meeting place."

The women's gate. It was embedded—quietly, obscurely—in the stone wall of the back court, on the Sabir Alley side. Except on Wednesdays, the men's end of our home, the Mahdi Street side, was forbidden territory for us women—from the front gate and court to the vestibule and the men's salon.

Mother's aggravation and Zaynab's frantic reassurances were understandable. My sister and I always had strict instructions to take the same route and never deviate from it. We were both fair-skinned and often mistaken for Italians, and our parents constantly dreaded acts of harassment or violence. Hence, Antar's protective ministrations and the unchanging route and routine, which started with the three of us going out through the back of the house—the kitchen and patio side, the women's gate side. That diminutive, unpainted, eyesore of a gate, studded with rusty nails that bled onto the weathered wood, was our inglorious egress into Sabir Alley and the flux of the real world.

From Sabir, we would direct ourselves toward Sidi Salem Alley, take a right turn there, and head south in the direction of the Atiq Mosque. At the top of Sidi Salem, we would turn right on Zarroog Alley, where our school was—nestled around a walled courtyard opposite the infirmary and a madrasa. While strategic Zarroog was the unofficial dividing line between the north and south ends of Benghazi's historic district, that corner location of Scuola Elementare e Media Giovanni Gentile marked the start of the east end, where the mesmerizing shops of Suq al Dhalaam beckoned, with the eastern half of Zarroog meandering through the motley labyrinths of our historic business district, all the way down to Piazza Fondouk.

But today was going to be different, and Mother was furious. We were to join our schoolmates and teachers by the fish market, and there was going to be a change in the initial part of our route. We had to explain—or probably justify—the switch, even though we had told Mother everything yesterday right after school. It was unusual for her to be cranky and strident, but the sleepless night had left her irritable.

"Damn these people!" she yelled.

"Don't worry, Mother. It's all very simple, really," Zaynab said.

"Well, no matter how simple it is, Antar will walk you to the fish market just the same—*and* wait with you till your teachers show their faces. These thugs have been nothing but trouble from the day they set foot in our country! Asking our young ones to go to the fish market on a school day!"

"It's not really the fish—"

"Enough quibbling!"

We put on our uniforms and coats, kissed our mother's forehead, and said goodbye to Auntie Mouna.

✼

My sister and I walked silently toward the designated meeting place, each of us lost in her own inexpressible thoughts. We had never even suspected the extent to which our parents and the older members of our family were agitated by this sudden turn of events. As far as I was concerned—although from the outset, I had a few qualms about taking today's unusual route—the Duce's visit was just another day at school. Even later, when I found myself on the high end of Piazza del Municipio with Signorina Cordini by my side, standing in the first row on that viewing platform, the child in me failed to realize how momentous the day was for the Italians, how high the stakes for everyone involved.

Soon, we joined our teachers and classmates, as planned, by the beverage booth opposite the fish market. Those of us who were given permission by their parents to attend stood there in the balmy sunshine and waited for Signora Taramelli—some thirty schoolgirls impeccably groomed and uniformed, bundled up in our superfluous coats, noisily curious and excited about this unexpected change in our routine. The four civilian-clad teachers who were in charge of us stood apart—they were silent and looked tense and broody.

Eventually, our principal showed up in a topless command car—black-uniformed and stunningly made up—next to an Alpini officer with a black raven feather in his forage cap. He pulled his car halfway up onto the curbed, European-style sidewalk, and she stood up and turned around instantly—looking at no one in particular, facing us once again from an elevated position with that ill-fitting garrison cap and that borrowed soldier's expression, her left hand gripping the molding of the windshield frame and her right raised in a Roman salute. The teachers returned her greeting with mechanical symmetry—including Mrs. Aswaani, who taught us Arabic. Then, without a word spoken, she sat back down in the passenger seat, and the two of them drove on toward Marsa Street, heading south in the direction of Piazza del Municipio. Our teachers now ordered us to form a column of twos, and we commenced to walk down Mahdi Street until we reached the north wall of our house.

We entered the north end of our historic district through the Turkish gate of Sidi Salem, with its impressive colonies of house sparrows nesting cleverly beneath the roof of the quarter, in the space between the gate arch and the eaves. The modern asphalt and roomy sidewalk of Mahdi Street gave way to the brick pavement and shadowy roofed alleys of the old city. The Italian teachers were now treading on alien territory, their familiarity with our quarter being limited to the highly visible, well-guarded stretch between Piazza del Municipio and the school on Zarroog. For my sister and me, however, this was our neighborhood, and as we marched into Sidi Salem Alley, I could hear Zaynab farther down the column behind me, already bragging, either to her mate or to Signora Cabrini, her custodian for the day: "The first whitewashed wall coming up on your right—you can't see much behind it, but that's the east wall of our house. The Moorish door next is ours, too. It's an annex—for our tenants, Mr. Sanz and his wife. He's an Andalusian shoemaker from Tunisia. They're going to move in next year. The closed door after that is going to be Mr. Sanz's shop. The restaurant to our left is Maltese—European, you know, but they can cook excellent Lebanese food for us. You just have to order it one day in advance. The big archway right next to it? That's a Moroccan tannery—thank God they keep all their stinky vats way back in the courtyard. The big shop to our right with the spice bags? My uncle's—Uncle Ibrahim. He has the best spices *and* the best honeys!"

Uncle Ibrahim. I saw him right there outside his spice and herb shop as we began to make our way up the alley amid the sweetly confusing aromas of Sidi Salem's north end—a redolence of European cooking overlapping with the spice scents and attars that wafted out of our uncle's shop. But something was deeply wrong with Uncle Ibrahim today: his expression was altered and strange—arms akimbo, feet firmly planted on the tiny sidewalk, as if he had been expecting this moment all along, waiting in a state of simmering, anticipatory anger for hours. I can still feel that moment with so much pain: it was the first time I had ever seen him enraged—and without his inseparable burgundy fez, which he always wore at a jaunty, flirtatious angle.

In my memory, our uncle's diminutive height and pencil-mustachioed appearance were permanently linked to a certain attitude of childlike cheer and clever playfulness. His face was endearingly ageless and moon-shaped, with those round tortoiseshell glasses only accentuating the cherubic chubbiness of his countenance, his otherworldly, dreamy eyes. In that instant, though, there were none of those familiar qualities in him, and I was once again baffled, failing to comprehend the intense, troubled emotions of an adult—that alien look on Uncle Ibrahim's face. For me, the expression of his eyes had always been a mark of warm indulgence and boyish humorousness, but today, those eyes seemed impenetrably hard or angry or desperate as he stood between the bags of spices neatly heaped and displayed on the wooden racks that flanked the doorstep of his shop. Stiff and on his guard in his work clothes—the traditional waist-length tunic and shalwar of drab canvas—he had an eerily clerical and bleak air, looking at us with what seemed like utter dismay or disgust. I couldn't help but feel threatened as we walked past his shop, and I looked back at him over my shoulder. That was when I saw him do it. In a fraction of a second, he snatched off his fez, looking even more threatening with his head bare, as if naked in his near baldness, cursing out loud in a deep, booming voice as he hurled it to the ground.

"May you be damned!" he growled after us, but we kept going, leaving him behind us as we walked on.

All the other men of Sidi Salem Alley appeared puzzled and vaguely titillated—these merchants standing outside their business establishments for the sole purpose of contemplating this surreal spectacle: a group of Libyan schoolgirls led by four women, three of them elegantly dressed and made up, disrupting their morning routine with the exotic, faraway scents of European perfumes.

Farther up on the right side of the alley, opposite the rug merchant, there was the Lebanese pastry store. Just as we passed it, I felt a hand on my shoulder and turned around without stopping. It was Auntie Fatima, the wife of the pastry chef. Walking alongside us, she handed me a few pastries neatly wrapped in notebook paper. I held the small package to my nose and gave her a grateful grin: bird's nest, my favorite pastry. It smelled just like their shop—roasted nuts, melted butter, and honeycomb mixed with the rug merchant's frankincense. I put the pastry in my school satchel. Through all of this, I kept walking—not out of rudeness but because I did not want to lose pace with Signorina Cordini, who kept walking mechanically, looking ahead in seemingly total indifference.

"For you and your sister," Auntie Fatima said, leaning over me and walking alongside me at the same time. "Have no fear. God is with you. He will give you strength, my darling little ones."

When we reached the intersection of Sidi Salem and Zarroog, we turned right, and our teachers told us to keep moving. It felt strange walking past our school without going in through the gigantic wrought-iron gate, just glancing through the gate's bars at the empty yard and the lone palmetto at its center, the budding mulberry trees at the back. There was a lot of bustle outside the infirmary opposite our school—a number of Bersaglieri soldiers in pith helmets and khaki uniforms frantically unloading boxes from a military truck and carrying them into the building.

By now, we could clearly hear the hum of the multitude rising over Piazza del Municipio—reverberations of a crowd stirring with excited anticipation, waiting. We walked on past the madrassa and up to the widening top of the alley where Zarroog made an elbow turn toward the south, sloping upward in the direction of the Turkish gate that opened onto a tiny yard behind our grandest mosque—the brow of the hillock forming the high side of Piazza del Municipio. Signorina Cordini ordered us to stop at the elbow turn and jogged up the steep end of the alley, standing a few steps inside the gateway. It was rather dim where we stood, and from our lower level, the only view of Piazza del Municipio was a patch of sky beyond the arc of the street gate—a seamless sheet of the purest, starkest indigo. It was a bright, balmy day, and the sweet intoxication of the season was in the air, in the moiling hum of the rally crowd just a few steps outside that gate.

Soon enough, we heard it—the signal from the middle of our town square: "*Plotoni Attenti. Uno, due, tre!*"

With mechanical precision, Signorina Cordini turned to face us, raising her arm and motioning us forward like a traffic policeman—our formal order to commence marching toward the viewing stand in the backyard of the mosque. The next thing I knew, Zaynab and I were out in the sunlight—hands held firmly by our two custodians—walking up a makeshift aisle with crowd-control barriers on either side of us. Only a few yards to our right, outside the forbidden perimeter of the mosque grounds, the crowd formed an unbroken blur of massed bodies pressed together all the way over to the Marsa Street edge of the square. The only distinctly visible thing on that side was the stand set up for the military band, which had been pitched in the middle of Marsa Street and stood almost as high as a shepherd's hut. My sister and I were the first among our schoolmates to be led up the shaky wooden steps of our stand. The rest of the pupils were still milling about in the yard as the two other teachers, positioned on either side of the steps, began forming them into two lines.

And now, I found myself standing high up on an empty platform—above everything and everyone, it seemed. The immediate perimeter of the mosque yard looked eerily deserted in contrast to the pressing throng on our right, which appeared disincarnate and foreshortened and oddly compressed, like a picture in a tiny slideshow camera. I turned around and looked down at the center of the square, feeling suddenly petrified next to my teacher, my senses stunned by the metamorphosis of the piazza into an unrecognizable theater of festive exuberance. After the relative quiet and dimness from which we'd emerged, this vast, blue-canopied square was almost unbearable in its brightness, its uproarious clamor, its motley mosaic of clashing colors, its frenzied human swarm. Everything was happening at once in this strange splinter of time—and so dazzlingly, so emotionally that it was impossible to see or guess which way the Duce had come. One moment he was nowhere to be seen, and the next, he was facing our mosque from the middle of the piazza, perched on a black Arabian stallion in his gray uniform and eagle-emblazoned cap, stone-still amid the hurricane of cheers and applause. The only other things that appeared to be quiet in this giddy moment were the monumental rectangular flags and banners that flanked the square on all sides, swaying against the Mediterranean sky like empty sails.

Now the military band to our right on the Marsa Street side—starchy, solemn, gray-suited, their black helmets shining with the gilded Fascist emblem—began to blare out one of the songs we had learned in school: "Giovinezza." The hailing men rimming the piazza from the sidewalks commenced to sing in one single, monumental voice, their arms stretched up and out over the crowd-control barriers like sticks and staves. The women waved their handkerchiefs over their heads as the men sang, and on the south side of the square, out by the podium opposite our mosque, a gigantic cardboard face of the Duce rose from among the crowd, towering above the bobbing heads with a huge caption in thick black letters painted across the Italian *Tricolore* underneath it: *W IL DUCE*. For minutes after that opening song, the crowd remained mad with enthusiasm, at times managing to orchestrate a spontaneous chant that rose up from them like the mammoth, two-toned retching of a gigantic beast: "DU-CE! DU-CE! DU-CE!"

The dictator remained unmoving amid the riptide of cheers, his mounted figure the monumental center of a huge human square within the square. Troops arrayed around him on all four sides—the men who viciously imposed his will and his power on our city: carabinieri, Alpini, and Bersaglieri in pith helmets, and the black-uniformed MVSN militia. The crowd howled hysterically, and the mounted tyrant remained stone-still within the neatly vacated area formed by his soldiers, facing our mosque as if in contemplation, his thumbs tucked under his belt, his uniform like a statuesque suit sculpted in brushed tin. Then came the long-awaited gesture: Mussolini pulled his "Sword of Islam" from its sheath and raised it above his head, in salute to the Cyrenaican chieftains who stood opposite him by the main stairs of the Atiq Mosque—"the upstarts," as Father angrily called them—the men who had just proclaimed him Protector of Islam in the secret ceremony. Shortly after his salute, the Duce dismounted, and with the crowd at a safe distance behind the barriers, he commenced to walk slowly toward the eagle-topped podium as the overlapping waves of mob madness crashed and echoed through the square.

That was when Signorina Cordini and Signora Cabrini signaled the two of us, Zaynab and me, to follow them. It was time to head back to our school. Flanked by the two women, we climbed down those unnaturally steep, unnervingly wobbly stairs and left our schoolmates with the other teachers. Back in the alley, the discordant clamor of the crowd raged like an unrelenting roar, but by the time we reached our school, a dead silence descended on the piazza—as sudden as the collective frenzy that had followed the dictator's appearance.

The four of us went inside the school and away from it all. My sister and I were more mystified than scared, but I was glad we had managed to walk away from the madness. There wasn't a living soul inside, and our deserted school grounds suddenly felt like a safe refuge from the chaos beyond the walls.

✧

Our teachers took us straight to the school nurse's office, where we were each given a stack of crisply folded clothes and asked to step behind a dressing screen to put on our welcoming-ceremony outfits. I called out to Signorina Cordini after a while, asking her to help me with the belt. She stepped in briskly and straightened it for me, adjusted my hair snood and blouse collar. Then she put her hands on my shoulders, leaning back and studying my appearance with her grave green eyes.

"Mariam," she said, "I could take you out for a stroll anywhere around the streets of Milan, and nobody would ever guess you weren't Milanese."

My sister and I stepped out from behind the screens. We stood before the mirror and contemplated our sudden metamorphosis for a moment. Our welcoming-ceremony outfits consisted of white, long-sleeved silk blouses with Peter Pan collars; white, black-buckled linen belts; and long black skirts.

"*La bruna e la rossa!*" Signora Cabrini exclaimed as we stood there laughing.

She went to fetch the welcome note and the Duce's gift while the two of us sat and waited by the nurse's desk. Signorina Cordini stood by the window, smoking and gazing absently into the courtyard. She had beautiful finger-wave-styled auburn hair and alabaster skin, and she bore herself with the exquisite grace of a dancer. But her ring finger was bare, and although she was always elegantly dressed, she rarely smiled and always stood alone in the schoolyard during recess—looking edgy and brittle-nerved, like an insomniac, chain-smoking with her fingers tapping on her thigh.

Our art teacher came back with the speech—a short text typed on a card—and a mother-of-pearl-inlaid rosewood box that she placed atop the desk, opening it and revealing a pair of black slippers embroidered with gold thread. As chance would have it, the leather used for those slippers had been tanned and dyed in the Moroccan tannery opposite Uncle Ibrahim's shop on Sidi Salem. After that, we headed to the refectory and had a full rehearsal of our role in the ceremony that lasted till around noon, when our classmates returned from the rally and joined us for a special lunch.

✻

And then he came—after the frantic preparations, the special school meal, the nervous waiting—chauffeured by a carabiniere in a convertible command car, followed by a large retinue of local officers, state officials, and public servants. The Duce left them all at the gate of our school and entered the court alone, followed by his secretary and the carabiniere, who remained discreetly behind in the dimness of the archway. Not counting the officer, the Duce was the only man in Scuola Elementare e Media Giovanni Gentile—the first man ever to set foot in our establishment during school hours. Signora Taramelli and another horrid woman in a similar MVSN uniform stood at attention by one of the inner columns of the archway, with our teachers lined up close behind them, followed by the nurse, the groundskeeper, and the cook. As for us pupils, we stood in the middle of the schoolyard, arrayed like troops, with my sister and me positioned distinctly apart in the foreground, next to a side table atop which the box was set. Keeping her eyes on the archway, Zaynab stood just a few steps before me with the card in her hand—her Andalusian back straight and slender and proud, her night-black ponytail glistening against the Italian shirt like a tassel of silk thread.

Signora Taramelli exchanged salutes with the Duce and addressed him briefly in words we could not hear. She then pivoted aside and introduced my sister, who, in our principal's words, had "written a short welcome speech for our Duce."

Zaynab snapped to attention like a soldier as Mussolini took a few oblique steps in the direction of our schoolmates, his black riding boots clicking against the cobblestones with a crisp, metallic echo—the unnatural dead stillness of a recess yard thronged with a platoon of perfectly lined up, utterly petrified pupils. His complexion was altered by a ruddiness that looked like a flush of latent rage. That was the first thing you noticed about him, along with the fixed expression caused by his chronic frown and the sag of his cheeks—a sad combination between a crybaby sulk and a disgusted wince that caused the skin of his face to droop on either side of his mouth. Mussolini had on the same military outfit he had worn during the rally—that bizarre, pewter-gray cap with the Fascist eagle and a matching uniform so stiff it looked like a tin suit and made him appear bodiless. He stood there immobile, barely a few feet away from Zaynab, contemplating our formation in silence.

Finally, he turned to look at my sister, and his face shifted into an incomprehensible expression—a discordant cross between a sour grimace and a smirk, as if he were unsuccessfully trying to pull a buffoonish face for Zaynab's amusement as she stood before him straight as a spear. Her crystal-clear voice rang out across the yard when she began to read the brief welcome speech in an Italian so excellent it made me glow with pride. And yet, to this day, I still cannot recall one single word from that speech, not that I was frightened—I believe I felt utterly incapable of fear—or even awed. In truth, my mental energies were simply too focused on the task at hand for me to grasp the details of what was happening before me. I lived the event as pure feeling—and the feeling I have retained from that moment is that of deep, warm pride at Zaynab's stunning achievement.

That achievement had apparently worked its way swiftly into the heart of the semi-clownish tyrant who looked so stiff and flushed, as if straitjacketed in his otherworldly uniform. He raised his eyebrows, popped his eyes wide, and gave my sister a deep nod of respectful admiration.

"*Brava, brava!*" he said emphatically as he drew near her. Then he took the few stiff, metallic steps that brought him before me and Signora Taramelli, who was now standing next to me and humbly asked him to accept "this modest gift from Scuola Elementare e Media Giovanni Gentile."

Before he even turned to face me, I grasped the inlaid box and stepped forward, holding it out on the flat of my palms, like a tray.

"*Grazie*," he said as he took it from me. "*Come ti chiami, piccolina?*"

"*Mi chiamo* Mariam Khaldoon," I replied, remembering that he did not bother to retain my sister's name and assuming he would not use my name when thanking me, too.

I assumed wrong, though, and was surprised when he repeated my name in Italian.

"*Brava, Miriam, brava*," he said as he opened the box and contemplated the gift proffered in the name of our school. The embroidered, butter-soft black slippers glistened with a dull sheen like two horns of onyx placed side by side on the burgundy-velvet lining of the box. The mystical forms of Berber embroidery glowed in gold thread like incomprehensible talismanic formulas.

He turned around and nodded at his secretary, who stepped up briskly, whispered a few words to Signora Taramelli, and took the box from the Duce.

※

Then he was gone—without bothering to listen to the songs we had so painstakingly rehearsed. Mussolini just faded out of our lives like a ghost, as senselessly and phantasmagorically as he had come. Followed by the tyrant's secretary and Signora Taramelli, that terrifying MVSN woman escorted Mussolini toward our principal's office, leaving us dazed and relieved and tired to our core—but also somewhat incredulous, as if we were all in doubt as to whether he had ever stopped by in the first place. My schoolmates were stunned and petrified, but they still remained respectfully at attention—until Signorina Cordini managed to shake herself out of *her* amazement, stepping up and announcing to all that the event we had put together went beautifully, that the Duce was very satisfied with Scuola Elementare e Media Giovanni Gentile. Unfortunately, she added, there was no time for the songs. He had to attend a brief meeting, then rush to Stadio Communale for the camelry parade and the equestran fantasia of the Berber horsemen.

Much to our relief, she released us early, and as we rushed out into the unusually crowded alley, my sister and I realized that Antar was nowhere to be seen. We walked home unaccompanied, ambling happily around the most out-of-the-way alleys, and as we stepped through the women's gate into the peaceful seclusion of the back court, Zaynab seized my hand, looking at me in silence for a few seconds—eyebrows raised, eyes wide open, her cherry-blossom cheeks slightly puffed out and her lips tightened together in a theatrically suppressed guffaw. She was rendering the facial expression of someone who was about to burst with laughter.

"Did you notice the horrible, horrible scandal?" she asked, recomposing her face into a cunning smile, whispering like a conspirator.

"What scandal?"

"Signora Taramelli is soooooo much taller than Musso-liiii-niiii!"

"That's right!" I screamed. "That's the first thing I—"

"Not so loud!" my sister whispered, tugging at my hand. "Not so loud. Those creepy MVSN crows are probably still spying on our house. Remember what Uncle Ibrahim said."

"That's exactly what I thought when she talked to him in the archway!" I whispered. "*She* should be the Duce. After all, she does have her own uniform."

My sister had a streak of wild playfulness in her that always reminded me of Ali. Taking her cue from my verdict, she stepped back, assumed a comically stern military expression, and raised her hand in the Roman salute.

"*Saluto a . . . Tara-melliiii!*" she said.

"*A noi!*" I replied—and we both exploded into laughter.

✣

Unfortunately, there wasn't much laughter for our family after that day—starting with Father, who soon began to sink into his private hell of implacable depression. From that spring of 1937 until his death, it seemed that his life was nothing but tormented, solitary brooding.

Before Mussolini's visit, my sister and I used to see Father once a week in the men's salon, on allowance day. Those treasured Friday mornings in the early and mid-thirties were the only times we were permitted into the benzoin- and sandalwood-scented male sanctum where he reigned supreme—the man we called Father: his sphinxian features (half Andalusian, half Phoenician) tightly framed by that perpetual scarlet fez; his black beard as dense and even as steel wool; his nose proud and elegant and straight, like the exquisite barb of an arrow carved out of sandalwood. The indirect manner in which I communicated with him during those sessions was similar to the way most girls of our class and upbringing spoke with their fathers: a very formal, very lopsided exchange within a setting closely controlled by Mother, who sat like an interpreter between the two of us during those Friday conversations. It was quite simply unthinkable for us girls to address our father directly. And so, everything I needed to say to the head of our family had to be carefully rehearsed with Mother before I sat down and faced him.

Loosely recollected, this is how one of those Friday sessions went—our exchange took place shortly before the tyrant's accursed spring visit:

MOTHER (*her face turned toward me*): Our little Mariam would like to tell you about some of the wonderful things she's learning in school.

(*I seat myself next to Mother, opposite Father, with the copper coffee table between us. I look at him—secretly, obliquely—sitting stiffly in his mother-of-pearl-inlaid armchair. His garden scent of apple-flavored tobacco and rosewater drifting on the air. His smiling eyes, an ambiguous shade of honey and brown clay, are statue-still and abstractly benign.*)

MARIAM: Gladly, Mother.

FATHER (*smiling, vaguely gazing into the interspace between Mother and me*): I trust everything is going well in the knowledge department—the most important of all after faith and family. A human being is not complete without knowledge.

MOTHER (*turning around to look at me*): Mariam's teachers are very satisfied with her. Tell your father, Mariam, what did Signorina Cordini say to Zaynab about you?

MARIAM (*face slightly bent, looking in Father's direction, barely containing my eagerness*): She said, "Mariam is a highly gifted pupil. She is precocious."

FATHER: Very good. Being precocious, as we all know, entails responsibility and hard work, of which you have your fair share. It pleases me greatly that you're a highly gifted pupil.

MOTHER (*smiling at him, proudly*): Sit Aswaani said the same thing. The most gifted student she'd ever had in Arabic, she said. Mariam, are you going to show your father the poem I helped you with?

MARIAM (*mock-shy*): Only with your permission, Father.

FATHER (*smiling*): Let's hear it. If it's perfect, you can show it to your teacher; otherwise—

MOTHER (*reassuringly*): Don't worry, I'll peruse it one last time before she takes it to Sit Aswaani.

FATHER: I'm not worried.

MARIAM (*reading out loud*):
Homeland, sweet homeland, dearest among nations!

You have my love, my longings, and my reverence.
I read about and tried to love other lands, other climes,
But my soul refused, finding solace in your sweet meadows alone.
Peace be upon you, upon the flower-specked slopes of your Green
   Mountain,
Its emerald woods, its azure skies, its snow-white waterfalls.
Peace upon its ancient, speared sentinels—wise and watchful.
Let the fragrance of my greetings mingle with your winds—
From this shore to the deepest depths of the sandy sea!

FATHER: Astonishing! We have ourselves a natural-born poet here—and an ardent patriot. *Mashallah,* Mariam! *Brahwa!* Your gift is probably inherited—we have a prominent poet on our side of the family.

MOTHER (*chiming in cheerfully*): And we have al-Hariri on *my* side of the family!

MARIAM (*heart racing, breathless, ignoring Mother*): Who is he, Father?

FATHER: She. An ancestor from Cordoba who lived in the Middle Ages—wrote memorable poetry and taught prosody. She was known as Bint Khaldoon al-Aroodhya. *Al-Aroodhya* means *the prosodist.* More recently, there is our beloved exiled family poet—Ahmed Mahdi, my dear cousin.

MOTHER: And al-Hariri. He wrote stories—very amusing, witty stories. A medieval man of letters.

The head of our family sat in his armchair like a monarch, beneath that most emblematic symbol of protection: his beloved damascene silver plate, adorning the wall with a hamsa sign at its center. We talked about my school achievements and our family heritage, and the conversation went smoothly for some time. It was a first: a Friday session fully dedicated to me and this other Khaldoon woman. I don't remember how long we spoke, but I can clearly visualize how humbly satisfied I was, just glad to be sitting there before Father, contemplating the distant glow of his barely contained pride—the tentative warmth of his oblique gaze, the uplifting power of his indirect words. And yet soon enough, there came that inevitable moment: Mother's formulaic announcement that it was time for me to stand up and take my allowance, which I did. Gratefully, deferentially, my head slightly bent forward, I stood up as I always did and tiptoed around the coffee table to take my money, kiss my father's hand, and walk out with Mother—never to set foot in the men's salon again until the next Friday.

✢

Then the tyrant came to town in 1937, and those strange, deeply treasured Friday conversations with Father came to a sudden, irrevocable end. In my memory, the interruption itself is, of course, one of the darkest moments of my childhood. But what hurt even more than the sense of personal doom surrounding our separation was the fact that I was not able to grasp the reason for his lofty silence. I did not know why I was sentenced to this hiatus, and I complained to Mother about it up to the last days of Father's life.

"He's upset," she would reply, her emerald eyes misting over, her face—my twin face—twisted with pain. Typically, after that helpless acknowledgment of my father's utter unreachability, his retreat into the dark recesses of depression, Mother would simply resort to her usual plea for divine justice.

"May God take revenge on you, Mussolini!" she would cry out.

So now, suddenly, jarringly, circumstances had imposed one more responsibility upon me, and emotional adjustments had to be made, if only to help myself cope with the harsh new realization gnawing away at me: that face-to-face Friday chat, furtive and frigid and formalized as it was, had now become a thing of the past—a self-indulgent luxury from which I had to learn to wean myself. Henceforth, my allowance would be handed to me by Mother every Friday—that much I knew for certain. Father had retreated into the shadows well before his passing, before the grinding force of history had turned him into another eternally displaced figure enshrined in a photographic portrait, next to Grandfather and Omar Mukhtar. One more monumental ghost among the restless, clangorous ghosts of the Resistance.

※

He was buried on March 26, 1939, and while our extended family gradually found a measure of peace—eventually coming to terms with the horror of his untimely death—the five of us were left with the lingering ache of his absence, which was, in many ways, far more terrible than the manner of his departure.

I never really thought of an alternative to the way he was—the way things were in those days for a father and his daughter—but it would be dishonest to say that those Friday glimpses of Father had never left me with a nameless sense of incompletion, or even emptiness, perhaps. It was always as if the entire experience had a certain power—independent of either of us—to make me feel helpless and small before this once irrepressible realization: the wordless awareness that although our Friday hour was so dearly desired, there was something about the space in which it took place that I found impossible to accept—a physical force, maybe, that invested the whole room with a primal power of impingement entirely detached from his personal beliefs or volition; a mute, relentless agency acting like a harsh and hostile environment fraught with elemental properties that were fundamentally toxic for both of us, as alien and unnatural to both our beings as the deep sea is to the novice diver. An environment, in sum, that contained none of the familiar substances of our world and that I took some form of eerie and irresistible delight in navigating, even though I knew full well that it was treacherous and impossible to trust and take for granted, inconceivable to settle in and call my own.

"*Mashallah*, Mariam! *Brahwa!*"

The only time I remember him saying my name.

※

I was still holding the last page of my husband's translation, still pondering my next move. Yet even as I was reading those terrible final words, I already knew how to begin Part Two: with Esther Sanz, of course—standing by her new house in the early spring of 1938. Esther and all the enchanting dreams that came hurtling into my heart the instant I saw her preparing to enter the home that my family had provided for her.

I put down the last page, picked up Basil's pen, and began to write the rest of my story.

The Night Visitor

For Aude Laloire

Poor Pauline: she just had to sit there and listen to me rehash the same story over and over again. I was in full monologue the whole time—out of fear, I guess; sheer, visceral fear, the kind of gut-level dread I was *trained* to overcome since my first day at karate school.

"I can't believe it," I said. "I'm always catching myself doing it, you know—thinking about him. I'll be in the middle of something, *anything*, and it'll just happen—the thought of him—like a power surge. It doesn't creep into my mind, or flash into my mind—or whatever. It just *happens*. Have you ever known me to think in circles like that? I mean, here I am, in the heart of *Quartier Latin* on a lovely fall afternoon, having a smoke with my best friend in our favorite café, and what am I doing? I'm actually discussing *him*. It's so weird."

"I'm telling you," Pauline replied, "there must be a powerful connection between the two of you—maybe a mix of fascination and repulsion. That's why I think you should see this woman. It may not be the only way to help you put this whole thing behind you, but it's a reliable way; you need to trust me on this. She'll give you an audiotape with your reading in it. It will help you unearth those dark, unconscious feelings and motives we all tend to bottle up."

"OK," I said, then paused, leaning forward slightly and looking her straight in the eye. "OK," I repeated, "but do I really want to do that? I mean, this isn't the sort of thing I'd want to do. God, Pauline! My father is the commander of a ballistic-missile submarine; my mother is a principal whose idea of a good time is to spend a whole afternoon rock climbing. All this New Age, crazy talk about consulting an astrologer who will dissect my unconscious motives with her occult powers is totally outside my frame of reference."

"But that's precisely why you should see her. Maybe you've reached a point in your life when you need to shake up your frame of reference. That's probably the hidden meaning behind this experience you've had. You should take it as a sign: you probably need to transition to a new plane of existence—something that's simply *you*, as opposed to your parents. I think this is a moment of self-renewal for you—an exciting plunge into the novel and unknown."

✻

Talk about a plunge.

It started in the summer of 2008—whatever *it* was—shortly before I decided (abruptly, chaotically) to move to America and become an altogether different person. Was it a glimpse of a new plane of existence? Probably. Something that's simply me? I didn't know yet.

I had just graduated from the Sorbonne and taken a position as a high school teacher in Paris's twelfth district. My parents had bought me a studio apartment in the fifth district—a graduation present.

It was, in other words, an exciting time. But it was also a period during which I found myself dwelling in the bliss of a pressure-free gap between two equally ebullient life phases. I remember spending the first two weeks of summer reveling in that hiatus: a lazy, laid-back interval between my last days as a newly graduated student and those tumultuous early-fall training weeks that mark the admittance of rookie teachers into the realm of public education. In other words, like my friends who had decided to go into teaching, I was determined to spend most of the summer not having to think about my next move—squeezing all the carefree fun out of those postgraduation days. I slept late every day, vegged out, went to the movies, caught up with friends, ate out a lot.

✻

Then came the day that changed all that.

My friend Tristan called from Quimper. His parents were giving him a combined birthday and graduation party.

"How about honoring us with your presence?" he said.

I told him I was going down to Cannes around mid-August—my kid brother's birthday party.

"When is *your* party?" I asked.

"August 12. Can you make it?"

"Yes, I can, but I'll have to leave the morning after. Are you inviting Pauline?"

"Yes, of course."

"Good. I'm actually taking her down South. I guess it'll be a Breton detour for the two of us, then."

"That's right. The rugged beauty of the Atlantic Coast before the exotic charm of the Mediterranean. Just make sure you book your flight out of Brest—I'll drive you. Would you like to come on August 10?"

We agreed on August 10. Then we chatted back and forth for a while, and I remember feeling unexplainably good about this spontaneous visit to my friend—an elusive mixture of excitement and tender nostalgia.

I should have known better, though.

Tristan is very into these RPG *events*, as he calls them. When he gets together with his friends, which he was planning to do after our visit, it would be nothing but role playing, literally from dusk till dawn. For days on end, these guys just vanish into another dimension, completely cut off from the material world inhabited by us earthlings.

Alternative mythological universes: that's where they all disappear when they play. And so, when I say I should have known better, I don't mean Tristan only; it's that whole thing about the RPG cultural milieu and the very peculiar characters peopling it.

Frames of reference again. In many ways, the cultural environment inhabited by Tristan and his crowd is diametrically opposite to mine: artsy types who get together and actually spend endless hours discoursing on the worlds where they plan to project their fertility goddesses and their virile gods in shining armor—the kind of worlds where Pauline would feel right at home.

Pauline. Now, how I got to befriend *her* is probably as much of a mystery as my friendship with Tristan. You cannot imagine two more different people—both physically and philosophically. She is, to use her terminology, the perfect "Venusian type": sensual, sweet, lovable at first sight—and just beautifully rounded; and I don't mean in body only. She also has well-roundedness in personality: fully developed emotional and social skills that allow her to empathize with those around her, to commune with them and radiate that unique aura of universal goodness she possesses.

Compared to her, I'm all sharp edges—literally and figuratively—about as sensual as a martial artist. That and my upbringing and I guess we can safely say I am not a traffic stopper.

Pauline keeps telling me I look great but have a poor self-image. "Your father," she says, "never helped improve your sense of self-love. All that karate and survival training should have been supplemented by a big dose of affection." I guess she's got a point there—I mean about my looks. Objectively, I'm supposed to be terrific in the looks department. I'm beautifully proportioned, elegantly tall and slender, with flaming auburn hair; and I have the greenest eyes you've ever seen. And yet I don't seem to be able to translate my beauty into some form of attractive image that I can project in the world around me.

One day Pauline made her definitive pronouncement on the image thing—a psychological diagnosis of sorts: "It's all about the aura you project and the vibes you send out," she said. "You're an amazing, drop-dead gorgeous girl, Nausicaa. All you need to do is work on your aura a little."

Good old Pauline. Aura and vibes. Maybe it was *that* damn mysterious.

※

Mid-August in Brittany: a spectral touch of chill in the air, the faintest hint of autumnal crispness. Those intimations of fall in the sea breeze are as close as you can get to the idea of a beautiful melancholy—the spirit of autumn already looming in the crystal air, lazy plumes of mist rising from the western rim of that cellophane sky.

There is nothing even faintly comparable to this in the South, where the blue of the August sky is much starker, much less ambiguous, and the air is heavy with sticky heat—the kind that makes you sluggish in body and in mind.

Those were my first unruly thoughts in Quimper, I remember; random impressions running through my mind on our way to the Galls' house. Mr. Gall ("Please call me Patrick!" he had insisted right after greeting us) had picked us up at the train station in a teal-blue Austin Mini—his wife's city car, he confessed defensively. Our host apologized for his son: Tristan was entertaining Marc, Audrey, and another guest, a friend from Bordeaux who had arrived shortly before us, apparently.

"The other RPG players will arrive two days after you leave," he added, probably to reassure us.

I was riding in the back seat and was able to appreciate the full extent of Patrick's massive back. He was huge—his big, round shoulders slightly hunched over the steering wheel, which he held like a plaything between his hands.

Patrick was talking to Pauline about Quimper—small talk, mostly—but his big, booming baritone got to me right away: it had that warm, unmistakably Breton touch. I don't know exactly, but it was the kind of voice that made you feel welcome from the start—as if you were returning home after a lonely journey.

Before long, we were parked in front of the Galls' place, a lovely, tiny 1920s' town house nestled, along with a couple of other homes, around a snug cobblestoned square: Wallace fountain purring away in the middle of it; lichen-mottled granite walls; quaint little balconies—their Quimper-blue, wrought-iron balustrades overflowing with bright-pink geraniums. Brittany at its best.

※

We found everybody in the kitchen: Tristan, his mother ("Please, call me Brigitte!"), Tristan's boyhood pal and RPG partner Marc with his girlfriend, Audrey.

And, of course, there was the other RPG devotee and family friend: Madani. He looked—there's no other way to put it—radically out of place in that kitchen; incongruous and unreal to the point of cognitive disconnection.

Don't get me wrong;, when I say he was out of place, I absolutely don't mean that with a racially biased connotation. Frankly, I tend to think of myself as having long outgrown the racism of my family—that of my Pied-Noir grandparents and relatives, specifically; my parents aren't racist, at least not consciously. Compared to the members of my generation, I am a genuinely post-racial woman—a point of pride with me, considering the terrifying ethnic uniformity of the environment in which I grew up.

I guess what I'm trying to say here is that I refuse to be held hostage to the imperatives of political correctness; not out of callous stubbornness, but because of the post-racial self-transformation I have been able to achieve over the years—gradually, arduously. What I want to do here is precisely give as unbiased a representation of Madani as I can, even while remaining fair to my subjective perception of the man. And so when I mention the incongruous sight of him sitting there in the Galls' kitchen, I don't intend it in a generic sense—that is to say, in terms of him being a *typical* fiftysomething Berber who is incongruously out of place in the company of *typical* Franco-French citizens.

What I mean is actually something that had to do with his *individual* look and attitude—or maybe it was the *air* that his look and attitude gave him; his aura, as Pauline might say. He radiated a certain kind of strangeness that just made him appear totally alienating and off-putting—there's simply no other way to say it.

But let me start with the hard facts and leave subjective impressions for later.

First, there was his physical appearance: You know The Twins in *Matrix Reloaded*, those braided henchmen the Merovingian unleashes on Trinity? He looked like them—only darker, chubbier, and with much coarser features. His waist-length, majestic dreadlocks were dyed a pronouncedly darker shade of brown than the hair on his scalp region—for dramatic effect, I suppose.

And then there was the T-shirt—a *black* T-shirt—stretched way too tight over his blubbery torso, if you ask me. An inscription was emblazoned on its front in scarlet Courier New Bold: "The Perks of Manhood."

At first I thought, *What the hell is that supposed to mean? Where are the perks, poor guy?* Then I saw the capper, and the thing began to make sense in its own oddball way: the colon after "Manhood." *All right, smart guy, I get it.* "The Perks of Manhood:" followed by black nothingness. Very funny.

To top it all off, Madani wore one teardrop pearl earring—the sort of thing you might give your grandmother for Christmas.

The tentacular hair; the in-your-face T-shirt; the clashing conservative earring. Talk about mixed metaphors. There was so much of the man's discordant oddness to take in all at once, it was mentally exhausting.

Funny how the human mind works: all these impressions racing pell-mell through my head while I sat there in the Galls' cozy kitchen—pleasantly sipping pastis and trading pleasantries; spending face-to-face time with one hell of a family friend: Madani the Berber calligrapher.

As my grandmother would say, life is one mighty mixed bag.

※

Ultimately, though, the real problem with Madani wasn't his appearance—or his aura, for that matter. It was the things he said and the way they interfered with group dynamics the whole time I was there.

I am fully aware that I'm treading on thin ice here. But precisely because I am, and because I am a post-racial woman who refuses to be held hostage to the imperatives of political correctness, I feel compelled to speak courageously and candidly: regardless of what the calligrapher said, or whether he was aware of how much nonsense he was dishing out, what I found deeply problematic was the insincere air of quasibeatitude with which everyone—except Pauline and me—greeted his comments. They were basically hanging on every word that tumbled out of Madani's mouth. It was as if everything he said—from a simple compliment to the most random, harebrained comment—was wisdom of the highest order.

I know this might sound ungrateful and unkind, but, in all honesty I must say that the general attitude toward Madani's peculiar behavior reeked of moral cowardice: It struck me as quite typical of a certain category of guilty leftists; and it's that kind of cravenness that drives me mad because it does *not* help the dynamic of race relations in this country—far from it.

※

So there I was, feeling conflicted from the moment I stepped into that kitchen; fretful despite all appearances to the contrary; secretly grappling with all these unspoken misgivings. And as the hours passed, I found the tacit interaction between Madani and the others increasingly irksome.

Now, Pauline has a completely different take on my unnerved response to the interaction issue. She thinks of it in terms of fate—a "karmically determined hate-and-fascination terrain," she wrote in one of the emails we exchanged after Quimper. A lot of nonsense, of course, and I've told her so more than once. The reason why the overall attitude toward Madani got on my nerves is very simple: unlike our hosts, I refuse to be held hostage to the imperatives of political correctness. Period!

Again, I will let the facts speak for themselves, starting with the calligrapher's misogynist vulgarity and how his friends reacted to it. Very soon after we got there, Madani began to expound on his theory of "the power of love," which, in his immense wisdom, he chose to illustrate by referring to the "burden a woman is willing to bear for the sake of love."

Initially, I didn't even understand what he was talking about—I mean *semantically*. What did he mean by "a woman accepting" to "bear a heavy burden" in order to "receive" love? It turned out the "burden" he had in mind was literal: one of the key indicators of "the power of love is that a woman, however physically fragile, is willing, in her quest for love, to have sex with a much heavier and stronger man."

To me, this rubbish would have been totally unacceptable from any other misogynistic man—and I would have given him a piece of my mind right then and there. But *this* man? He was just too pitiful for words. *Poor guy*, I thought, watching him make an ass of himself with his theory of no-weight-class erotic wrestling. But this was apparently all right with everyone else—except for Pauline, who was just as bewildered as I was.

Rest assured that I have no intention of taking you on a tour through the Madani Blooper Gallery. What I want to do here is show you that for all his acquired veneer of glib eloquence, the calligrapher from Bordeaux was a constant source of embarrassment, because what he said either didn't make sense or was socially inept.

I must also add that if I found myself suddenly smoldering in that kitchen, it wasn't out of uptightness, or priggishness, or whatever it is that gets people ruffled when they're confronted with such gratuitously shocking conversation topics. Although I *am* a prude when it comes to expressing my feelings, I am ultimately the kind of prude who, given the proper circumstances, will manage to put on a brave face and engage in a mature discussion about such things.

As I said, though, what unnerved me most about Madani's outrageous comment was his hosts' failure to identify it as such and immediately ask him to tone down his language and his attitude. Instead, they kept nodding their heads with those phony, PC smiles I hate so much.

※

Madani did more than talk nonsense in the kitchen, though. That evening, assisted by Patrick and Tristan, he cooked the most delicious couscous I had ever eaten. I say this as someone who is well-versed in the art of making couscous: my Pied-Noir grandparents were born in Algeria and, true to family tradition, my father had learned to make great couscous himself: fish couscous, vegetarian couscous, sweet couscous. But the dinner that man put together was something I had never experienced before. The food was so good, a reverent hush fell over the table as we began to eat.

Eventually it was Brigitte who broke the silence, complimenting Madani and telling him what we were all thinking—namely, that this was an exquisite couscous.

"It's the sun," he responded, another of those senseless telegraphic statements he had an unhappy knack of often blurting out.

"The sun?" I asked, in an attempt to help him help us make sense of what he was trying to say.

Deliberately ignoring me, he explained to Brigitte that the semolina was prepared by his sister and her friends: "Hand-rolled, then sun-dried. There's nothing like sun-dried couscous. All the sun packed into those semolina grains—it gives your couscous a unique, rugged fragrance that fills your kitchen with goodness as soon as you start steaming it. Now you all know: the African sun actually does have an aroma."

More phony PC smiles!

※

After dinner and dessert, we sat around our hosts' Asian coffee table drinking aged rum. The liquor made me a bit light-headed and aggravated the stress and fatigue clashing inside me, the jumbled impressions of the day. It was time to go to bed.

The day he had called to invite me, Tristan had told me to bring a tent—because of the size of the house and the shortage of rooms. Now, tent bag in hand, I wanted to know about our sleeping arrangements.

Tristan got up and walked over toward the living room sliding glass door with the two of us in tow. He switched on the garden lights and we followed him through the door onto a small deck with a flight of stacked-stone stairs leading down to a pretty little sunken garden.

"Watch out for the rosebush," he said over his shoulder as he led the way.

We went down the stone stairs behind Tristan, and soon enough the three of us began to pitch the tent.

After that Pauline and I went to the upstairs bathroom, then back inside our newly pitched tent, whereupon, just as we started laying out our sleeping bags, I remembered we hadn't said good night; so back up those rugged garden stairs we went. The living room slider was left ajar—Brigitte's instructions—and we pushed it open a little bit more, peeking in to wish them goodnight.

"Off to bed already?" Patrick boomed from the couch with that warm, resonant voice.

"Oh, yes!" we chorused.

But I was unable to fall sleep—so many things racing through my mind—and although it was pitch-dark inside the tent, Pauline had immediately picked up on my confused feelings. "You can't go to sleep?" she asked with an affirmative hitch in her voice, as if the question was purely rhetorical.

"No. Serves me right—this happens when I don't write in my diary before bedtime. I kind of feel guilty about it—maybe."

She flipped the clip-on reading lamp switch and propped herself up on her elbow. I was on my back with my face turned toward my friend, looking up at that lovely, alabaster countenance with a strange and sudden feeling of relief—those gorgeous locks of dark hair dangling down the right side of her face. But the sensual roundedness was nearly gone from Pauline's features: there were deep, dark lines around her mouth and eyes and I found it difficult to read her mind. Her bow-shaped lips looked diminished and shrunken in the feeble light. She had an expression that was either grave or sad; it was hard to tell.

"What is it?" I said, as if *she* was the sleepless one.

"Madani," she said.

"Tell me, what's your impression of him?"

"He's burning."

I don't know why, but my heart skipped a beat at the sound of those words, and I actually visualized the man burning—his matted locks ablaze like kerosene-soaked ropes.

"What do you mean, *burning*?"

When I uttered those words, I think I was feeling rather unsettled—vicariously, I suppose. Now that it was time to go to sleep—after the delicious couscous, the mellow after-dinner conversation and the pleasant rum—my best friend was suddenly, uncharacteristically aloof and unfathomable in her pensiveness, the isolation and foreboding in her voice, the cloud of torment stealing over her face.

"I don't know," she said. "He looks like he needs to do a lot of self-healing. I think there's a lot of hurt or anger inside him."

"Frankly, I don't think there is any 'hurt' or 'anger' inside him, as you put it. All I see is a lot of immature showboating."

"Nausicaa, you're being too hard on him. That cocky attitude is a mask he wears to face the outside world."

"A mask? Are we talking about the same person here?"

"No, we're not. It's all just a show, you know; an act he puts on to hide this ... deep-buried hurt I can't quite put my finger on."

"Honestly, all I see is a man who's probably too complacent for his own good. You're being so hyperbolic, Pauline. It's not like you. Don't forget, *I'm* the Southerner here; hyperbole is *my* specialty."

"It's in his eyes, Nausicaa. Watch his eyes: they're so much at odds with his attitude. They have this rhino ... this inert, vortexlike depth about them—like an opening into a deep well of nameless pain within him."

"Those are wrinkles, Pauline. Patrick has them, too, you know. It's called aging. I think you're projecting way too much poetic grandeur onto the guy, turning him into some kind of tragic hero. You only had *dinner* with him!"

Pauline looked down, and her eyes seemed lost in somber thought. When she spoke again, her gaze was still lowered, and she sounded as if she was ignoring me—or whispering to someone behind her in the tent.

"You're being captious—using my words against me. It's the *expression*. I'm talking about the hidden expression *behind* the wrinkles. And the depth in his eyes: that depth isn't introverted depth, or dreamy depth, and it's not wise depth either. The man has been through so much pain—I can *feel* it. I don't know; maybe a terrible series of betrayals, maybe abandonment or hatred."

"And that's why you feel sorry for him? For having endured a lot of *hypothetical* pain? There's no reason for you to feel guilty—I mean if the guy is so screwed up. There is such a thing as personal responsibility, you know."

"I'm not guilty—and I wish you wouldn't say such things," Pauline replied, more abstracted than irritated—her voice tired and sullen, secretive and withdrawn.

She rolled over on her back, slipping her arms into the sleeping bag without looking at me. I sensed a hint of impatient finality in the movement. Was she getting upset?

"I didn't say I felt sorry for him," she added in a hoarse whisper. "You're banalizing my words. I'm saying that his eyes reveal a lot of vulnerability, and *because* of that, he radiates an aura of hurt. Are you getting sleepy now?"

Now I knew I *had* upset her. I flipped over on my side and tried to smile in the light. "I'm sorry I upset you."

She gave me back a pale smile, pulled her hand out of the sleeping bag, and tapped me on the shoulder. "You didn't. I'm just exhausted—that's all."

※

The next morning we had an early breakfast and headed out to Bénodet, while Patrick and Brigitte slept in.

We drove out with Tristan in Patrick's BMW—Madani, Pauline, and me. Marc and Audrey followed behind us in Brigitte's car.

The weather couldn't have been lovelier—dry, moderately hot—and we went straight to the wooded country southeast of Quimper for a trail hike along the Odet River and a lunch of crepes and local cider in an old riverside inn.

After that it was back to the country road and the ride to Sainte-Marine bay: The quaint, nineteenth-century brick-and-stone canneries outside the fishing hamlets; the eighteenth-century monastery sprawled high atop the wooded hills; then the final stretch and the breathtaking drive over the causeway—the always too-sudden-to-take-in, always too-beautiful-to-believe cyan dazzle of the bay flashing in sight, with the lazy river flowing emerald into it. And the unreal, toylike "Rooster Lighthouse" of Bénodet perched on the promontory—standing oddly low for a lighthouse, its high-gloss white and green reflected in the plate-glass stillness of the water.

My mother is Breton and we used to come up here often when I was a child—it is country I know and love—and so as we glided down the causeway and turned beachward after the traffic circle, it felt like coming home.

※

Things didn't go too well at the beach, however.

As soon as we got there, Tristan treated me to a brief but annoying one-on-one lecture—on the fine art of inclusion, I suppose. He said he had a feeling Madani was becoming increasingly aware that he was getting the cold shoulder from Pauline and me. It seemed the calligrapher went so far as to tell him, Tristan, that his friends from Paris weren't being particularly friendly, despite his many attempts to engage them in conversation.

I said, "Well, you know how I am, Tristan. You should have told him I need time to warm up to people. Actually, now that you mention it, I'm not sure I could ever warm up to Madani's conversation starters. In fact, everything he says is abrupt, weird, and off-putting. Also, I think Pauline finds him a tad too intense, and you know how *she* is—so I'm also being protective of her. I guess some of that, too, must have come out in my attitude."

Eventually, we all went for a swim, Tristan obviously not too happy about my response to his windy pontifications and me thinking, *Oh well, he'll get over it.*

※

Then there was the underwater thing.

I don't even know how much of it actually happened. Strange how memory functions and malfunctions, how often we take its workings for granted. That it is selective is to be expected, of course, but when you find out the arcane mechanisms of recollection—the cutting and pasting, the highlighting and adumbrating, the deleting and inserting—operate in ways that are totally alien to your understanding of what remembrance itself means, the realization that you're grappling with a different animal altogether leaves you forever changed.

At any rate, whether the underwater thing did or did not happen, this is how I recall it. I remember us frolicking in the shoal at first, and then eventually swimming out into deeper water. That's when I decided to indulge in an old childhood game: playing at going down beneath the surface, sinking deeper and deeper into the water—feet first, with my eyes closed, letting myself go with the sheer joy of this miraculously warm and gentle day, feeling the seconds tick off inside me before my feet hit the sand. And then it just happened: for some utterly unfathomable reason, I opened my eyes as I kept plummeting downward and saw something above me that rattled my entire being. I caught an electrifying glimpse of Madani gliding underwater, sleek as a seal. The impression was so powerful that when I closed my eyes again, the glow of the afterimage was like a phosphorescent figure etched on my eyeballs—the tangle of dreadlocks undulating around his head like snakes sucking on his skull; the blubbery, phocine slickness of his hairless torso; those crazy purple sprinter shorts from the eighties—fluttering like a damn plastic bag caught around his waist (that miserable, luckless Berber wanderer hadn't even had enough sense to pack a pair of swimming trunks).

It was all too much to take—our desert hero making an appearance like that. All at once, something just snapped inside me, and for a split second I thought I was on the verge of heart failure. My first instinct was to swim up to the surface and head back to shore as fast as I could. Very soon, though, I realized I wasn't breathing right and began to wonder if I was actually having a panic attack. I decided to float on my back for a few minutes and let go of the fear first—drift slowly away from the others and recover my wits bit by bit. I'm sure that sudden fright wasn't some sort of irrational revulsion toward Madani or anything even approximating that. In many ways, what I felt—and perhaps even what I saw—had nothing to do with Madani at all. Some deep, primal psychological mechanism in me must have gone haywire, signaling an unidentified animal threat—and that was why my entire system went into flight mode. Anyway, as soon as I was able to pull my thoughts together, I began to swim slowly back toward the beach. Before long, I was wading the shallows.

⁂

Later that day, after dinner, there was Patrick's wonderful rum again and a calligraphy slideshow—the high point of the evening.

Madani's calligraphy: breathtaking even onscreen. After the show, we leafed through a few of his books—the printed ones and what he called, in his bizarre French, the "bouquets," by which he meant the one-of-a-kind, albumlike books of original calligraphies executed on cotton paper and thread-bound by him. (I bought one of his "bouquets" that same evening—an indulgent graduation present to myself.)

Not being at all familiar with the ancient art, I cannot comment on his style with any degree of expertise. This much, however, I will say: Madani's work is clearly more than an attempt to express consummate calligraphic virtuosity in all its forms. It's far more daring and ambitious than that, as it seeks to chart unknown artistic territory, to open up esthetic and expressive avenues that stretch far beyond the trite, all-too-pat arabesque sensuality you find in the more conventional works of Arab calligraphy.

Stroke after stroke, Madani's script unfurls on the page in wild, loosely structured clusters of whirling curves—broad and dense-hued at their inception, then tapering off into thin traces of scattered color gradations, like comet tails or the stippled trails from a burst of fireworks. It is all so beautifully executed—a gorgeous choreography of controlled chaos; the energy explosive and measured at once—caught in its downward momentum, its tight vortices of burning pain and passion that trail off into scatterings of vanishing color sometimes as frail and ethereal as stardust.

In the collection I bought from him, *The Book of Love*, the word "Love" is placed in the center of the first page, followed by an epigraph inscribed underneath it in traditional calligraphy—very thin, interlaced scarlet letters resembling a seal. The translation in the glossary reads as follows:

> *Boy, my longing has become clamorous,*
> *My drunkenness goes beyond all bounds:*
> *I need a jug of wine and a book of poetry,*
> *Half a loaf for a bite to eat,*
> *Then you and I, seated in a deserted spot,*
> *Will have more wealth than a Sultan's realm.*

That single word penetrates your entire being as swiftly as an epiphany: the word "Love" drawn in imbricate strokes of slate gray and fiery rose on a very subtle ground of diffuse, opalescent blue. The overall effect resulting from the interplay between inscription and ground is a shifting, abyssal gape in the middle of the page—a convoluted maelstrom of smoke and ardent volcanic fire against an indifferent, placid horizon of misty iridescence.

The grounds he created were always elaborately set up for these whirling dances of color and form: If you look closely behind the words, you will realize that the field of color opening out beyond is meant to trick the eyes with its nearly invisible curves and layered folds of fine-textured, foggy hues—as if the words themselves have risen out of a storm-swept landscape of dunes or between the barely perceptible swells of a nebulous sea.

✤

Feverish impressions of my day at the beach still running pell-mell though my mind, along with the rum, the slideshow, and the books. I found myself once again feeling overwhelmed, weary to the bone, and somehow ill at ease—troubled by the nagging thought of an odd, nameless stiffness in my body.

I wanted to withdraw to a faraway place in my mind, lie curled up and peaceful in bed. And that was exactly what I told everyone. I said it was time for me to turn in—abruptly, a tad rudely perhaps. Much to my surprise, Pauline said that she, too, was tired—although I suspect she was going along with me out of politeness, to smooth out the awkwardness of the moment.

I went to the upstairs bathroom before her, and when I came down and said good night, I even forgot to thank Madani—for the show, for the book, for the stuffed peppers and all the other things he had so generously shared with us. It wasn't until we were both in bed that I realized the extent of my gaffe and how upset Pauline was. When she switched off the light, I asked her if she thought there were influences of Asian calligraphy in Madani's work. Gauging her mood.

"You could have asked *him*, you know."

That was when everything came to a head—the retort that spiraled out of control and became the culmination of our strange, exhausting day.

"Excuse my bluntness, Pauline, but have you just snapped at me?"

"No, I haven't. I was just saying that of all the people there you were the only ... I just want to say that you bought his book, and yet you didn't even bother to ask him a single question, which is perfectly all right with me. If you're not—"

"No, it's not that I'm not. I *am*, as a matter of fact. I just—"

"Listen," Pauline said. Then she sighed and stopped, as if she was actually trying to listen to something outside.

Suddenly, I could feel it—her agitation hovering in the vaulted dark above us, like a nauseous emanation. *Poor thing*, I thought, *she's very upset; tired too.*

She said, "You know, you're being... Can we give it a rest?"

That was Pauline all right—her way of showing deep upset. I knew what I had to do. "Absolutely," I replied, and I rolled over and lay curled on my side.

Enough said.

※

What happened over the next few hours was the stuff of magical realism fiction—an outlandish concatenation of events that threw me into utter disarray.

Sometime in the middle of the night, I managed to slip out of the tent and creep into the house—in my sleep. I was able to open and fasten back the tent flap, step over the stakes without stumbling or tripping on the guy lines, duck under the thorny branches of the sprawling rosebush and negotiate the deck stairs without a single scratch or misstep. I then pushed open the already ajar sliding door, waltzed through the living room without upsetting a thing or stubbing my toes—or worse.

Then I was able to creep up the stairs to the bedrooms. When I reached the landing of the first story, I lay down on the parquet floor and fell into a deep slumber—right outside the calligrapher's room.

And that was how Brigitte found me when she came down in the morning. (Later, as the two of us sat down to breakfast, she laughed and told me how "cute" I looked—curled up with my back against the door.) But now, as she stood at the bottom of the second flight of stairs, trying to decipher my fate, Tristan's mother seemed more compassionate than amused; the expression on her face tinged with a hint of sadness, probably because she was struggling with slippery thoughts she preferred not to spell out to herself—at least not now, on this morning of all mornings. After all, today was the high point of the visit: the day we were celebrating her son—his coming into the world, his rise in it. There was definitely no time for a bleary-eyed, washed-out woman who didn't have enough sense to stay put in her tent.

To this day I still cannot quite grasp the intent of those sad-smiling blue eyes: Was it wise empathy? Was it pity?

Brigitte spoke softly. "I'm going to make some coffee," she said, with her hand on the newel finial and one foot still dangling playfully over the edge of the bottom step as she contemplated me.

The instant she uttered those words, something in me began to come alive, and I immediately felt the pain in the nape of my neck. Even as I tried to comprehend the meaning of her presence here before me, I realized the back of my head was literally wedged between the parquet and the door panel. I sat up and tried to push myself upright, but I couldn't—my elbow was as stiff as a stick. Brigitte sprang off the step at once, giving me her hand, and as I stood up, I began to face her more squarely—my gaze less diffuse and yet even more mystified than a moment before, as if, for some very unpleasant reason, she was behind all this—whatever *this* was.

I wanted to say something, but then I thought better of it—after all, there *was* nothing to say, really. I had never felt more confused in my life. Actually, for a harrowing second there I found myself wishing I was still asleep. I began to feel dizzy and so I stepped up closer, put my hand on her shoulder to steady myself, and closed my eyes. I opened them after a few seconds but was still feeling dizzy and had to close them again. I started to register the pain in my bones, too.

Brigitte had read the frailty of my body and my face right from the start—that first look of naked bewilderment in my eyes, the raw vulnerability of people who turn into strangers to themselves. And now she wanted to reciprocate my intimacy and help make sense of this. Gently, she put her hand on my back and pulled me toward her. I let my face rest on her shoulder. "Don't worry," she whispered, "it's nothing serious. You were just sleepwalking."

※

So now you know all about it—this story of the vacation from hell; of the girl who wound up sleeping on the first-floor landing of a home she barely knew—one flimsy door between her and a man who probably slept like a beached dolphin.

During the weeks that followed my sleepwalking episode, Pauline had gradually developed a very creative interpretation of what had happened. Calling this "highly revealing" event a sleepwalking episode, she argued, was a "reductive" way to come to terms with it. A "karmic signal": that was the name *she* had for it. Hence the impassioned debate about the astrologer at the *Quartier Latin* café—a debate I ended up losing to my infinitely endearing, patiently persuasive friend.

And so, against my better judgment, I ended up agreeing to consider it—sitting down with her stargazer in order to decipher the meaning of what had happened that night. Pauline was thrilled—pumped up on caffeine and sanguine. At the end of our conversation, she even told me about a woman who stole into her next-door neighbor's apartment and spent the remainder of the night sound asleep in his living room.

I laughed. "Great! Another night prowler. I should place an ad and found my own society—The Order of the Night Visitor."

Pauline must have mistaken my nervous laughter for mockery. When she retorted her tone was both caustic and disapproving, in a moralizing way. "You know, I hate to spoil your fun, but the woman in question actually ended up dating the neighbor."

When she saw the expression on my face, she blushed. "No, no, no, no, no! Please let me be clear that I'm *not* rushing to any conclusions about secret attractions here. What I'm trying to do is find a frame of reference—a form of interpretive model. There was something karmically (existentially, if you will) crucial that this woman didn't consciously know about regarding her relationship with her boyfriend—or her neighbor, for that matter. Sleepwalking was the fated warning that revealed that something; and when she was done processing the whole incident, she knew it was time to wake up and face reality. This is not to say that you're in a similar situation. What I'm talking about here is the general *process* of learning itself—independent of the specific *content* of the lesson. You tell me you've been a sleepwalker since childhood, and I get it. But *this* particular sleepwalking episode is specifically significant: It's asking you to learn about hidden aspects of your persona—facets of your inner self that you have probably put a lot of time and energy into evading."

That night, I sat down and mulled the whole thing over, and when I was through thinking, I had resolved to see the astrologer. Maybe consulting the stars *was* the only way to get to the bottom of this insane story—come to terms with it, in PaulineSpeak. Maybe a crazy solution was the only way to deal with a crazy problem.

⁂

She was a very elderly woman—blindingly blond hair, turquoise eyes, heavily tanned—and she introduced herself as Isis. She kept calling me "young lady," and I hated her for that right from the start. I also hated everything she represented and everything she said—right from the start.

She switched on the tape recorder and said, "Young lady, do you know what they call fate in the Maghreb?"

I said I didn't.

"One of the Maghrebi words for fate is *maktoob*. In our language, it means 'that which is written.' So, here we are, Nausicaa Durand, launching forth upon a reading of your *maktoob*—the meaning of this encounter that fate intended as a token and a warning."

All the signs were there, she said: the relationship chart she drew up based on his and my birth data indicated "a fated relationship, a deep relationship, a relationship with immense potential for self-fulfillment—a relationship that should not be taken lightly. And yet it seems that something in you is resisting the constructive challenges this man is bringing into your life, the—"

"I am *not* resisting him," I almost shouted. "I had nothing to do with him. I'm not even supposed to *remember* him!"

She looked away for a few seconds, and when she resumed, she spoke with strained deliberateness at first. "You see, that's probably the root of the problem. You say you are not supposed to remember him. Did you ask yourself why? Maybe somewhere within you this man represents the forbidden, which in turn feeds into the basic attraction that was there in the first place. Young lady, if you keep going down the path of denial, I don't think you'll be able to *stop* remembering him—if that's what you really want. If I were you, I'd try to email him instead—see what happens. No particular design, no expectations. Just get to know him; maybe ask him a few questions about his calligraphic techniques, his inspiration, and so on. Familiarity is the best remedy against fascination."

By now I was in a smoldering rage. This whole thing was completely unreal, like a dream in which you find yourself going through the motions of an insane farce; and she was a total fake—with her hackneyed, New Age mumbo jumbo about fate, her cheap, suffocating incense, her cheap oriental knickknacks, her cheap jewelry twinkling all over her like tinsel trinkets.

"But there *was* no fascination," I told Isis, as if pleading with her. "There isn't any fascination, and there *won't* be!"

Isis must have been both upset and taken aback by my outburst. Her jaws clenched and her face was suddenly inanimate and hard and dark, like a sinister papier-mâché mask. She looked away again, and there was a moment of silence during which she bit her lower lip hard, barrel-distorting the lipstick feathering below her vermilion border.

This time I think I had come very close to shouting, and I turned and looked at Pauline, like a nervous reflex. She looked positively appalled, her cheeks burning with embarrassment. Suddenly, I began to feel guilty and exposed; after all, I did promise her to make nice and play along—approach the whole thing in a humorous, laid-back spirit of experimentation. Yet here I was, acting boorish and putting a well-intentioned friend—the best I had ever had—in a mortifying position.

"All right," Isis said from behind her gigantic Louis XVI desk and fell back into silence.

I turned to face her again, and in the dark, smoky room it was like looking at her for the first time: She didn't seem so much remote as fogged over—as if she was speaking from behind an impalpable veil of opacity, a sort of animated torso addressing me through an infinitely tenuous pall of mist.

"Listen, why don't we first agree on some . . . basic rules of communication, all right? Right now I'm wondering about something, and I'd like to share my thoughts with you for a minute. Would you like to do that?"

"Yes."

"Good. I'm trying to think of a way we can do this reading with as little tension as possible, and you know what? Maybe we should both think of it as a *game*. Do you think you'd like to—enter into the reading with that sort of spirit? Think of it as a game?"

I managed to squeeze another "yes" out of myself. Suddenly, I realized how parched I was—my throat felt like a cardboard tube. I swallowed, pressed my tongue against my palate, and asked her if I might have a glass of water.

She brought me a cool bottle of Evian and I took my first sip. Then she commenced the reading.

She said I was to sit back and listen at first, which I did. I was already feeling very tired—a deep-seated, bone-anchored fatigue. The tension of holding still, I suppose. Bone-tired—now I understood the real meaning of that word. I was definitely that, and she wasn't through with me yet.

⁂

When she came to the section in her notes that dealt with me—as opposed to the section about me and Madani, a subject I don't want to go anywhere near here—she began to elaborate on my fear of commitment.

Isis told me that the fear seemed to originate in deep-buried memories of my mother; she said that maybe as a child I had felt that she—my mother—was probably not fulfilled in her marriage; that her full potentials were possibly "blocked" *by* the marriage in some way.

Blocked potentials? Silently, stubbornly, I disagreed with her. And yet I did find myself remembering something along those lines while she rambled on.

My mother seething with anger, staring right down into my eyes: I was just a kid, maybe seven or eight, and we were vacationing on the Breton coast, not far from Quimper. I had skinned my elbow slipping on a slimy rock and ran toward her, crying. She stood up and rushed in my direction, meeting me halfway.

I guess I was expecting consolation, concern—the emotional response a child of that age expects in that type of situation. Instead, she just flew into a rage, kept glowering at me from up there—her gigantic maternal heights. "This is the second time, the second time, you come to me whining like this. Listen carefully, Nausicaa: in this life there are two kinds of people, the whiners and the winners. And it's up to you to decide which you want to be. If you want to be a whiner, you're going to be stuck with your helpless, miserable whimpering for the rest of your life, and I won't be able to help you with *that*. You know why I can't help you? Because it's up to *you*, and you only, to shake yourself out of it and be a winner. Now, tell me which one you prefer to be: a whiner or a winner?"

She actually made me say it, right then and there, skinned elbow and all. She made me decide that I didn't want to grow up to be a whiner; that I was going to dedicate myself to being a stiff-upper-lipped, stick-it-out-come-hell-or-high-water winner.

I suppose you might say that by then she had made her point, the ego contest—if you can call it that—having gone her way. But no; her face kept turning redder and redder as more thundering followed. My mother was simply boiling within—her soul inhabited by something disproportionate and distempered beyond words, something I found utterly unfathomable. Still, I remembered how after that confrontation I was capable of stepping back from the moment and concluding, with a deep sense of pity, that this wasn't about me—that something far bigger, far more convoluted was eating my mother up inside.

Eventually, I came to know just what that something was, and how much it had to do with my mother's sense, repressed mostly, of being trapped—trapped and helpless. Obviously, I have no intention of going into *that* now, it being another story—Mother's story and hers alone.

※

Even as Isis droned on, expounding on my relationship with my mother in hieratic, New Age mumbo jumbo, I found myself remembering something else, another defining moment in my life—an event that, despite its seeming banality, had cut a long path of desiccated desolation through my utterly confused teenage soul.

It was a judgment my mother had made in connection with my maternal uncle's separation from his wife up in Limoges. She had told me the separation was going very poorly, and that she didn't approve of the way her brother was handling the situation—an understatement, I assumed. I listened dutifully but absentmindedly for a while, then started shuffling out of the kitchen; and that was when she threw it at me—one of her freeze-in-your-tracks sentences. "Anyway," she went on "when all is said and done, men and women simply are not meant to live together under the same roof."

Once again, it dawned on me that her comment went well beyond the here-and-now context. This time, though, I was good at figuring out the causalities and the ramifications—far better than the scrawny, confused eight-year-old girl on that Breton beach. Just the same, though, I was a teenager, with heaps of starry-eyed notions about guys; and despite the fact that I could have used a big dose of realistic enlightenment in the boy department, a significant part of me desperately wanted my notions to *remain* starry-eyed. Heaven knows I wasn't ready for such desperate, hard-core statements—and from my own mother to boot. I just didn't know what to do. For days on end, those words kept echoing in my head like a death sentence.

My mother and her blockages—tell me something I don't know.

※

I have no idea what it's like to be kicked out into the street right after major surgery. Yet it's the only image I can think of to describe my state as I took my first steps out in the street with Pauline by my side. Raw: that was what I would have said if I had to put a name to the state of my body and my soul in those moments—walking around and feeling as if the sum of my being was a raw wound.

It was another ravishing Indian summer day in the very middle of Paris—the heart of Montmartre. In its decline, the sun cast its last ruddy rays on the limestone walls—a time of day in this quarter when you could easily trick yourself into believing that some of the old buildings looked like ancient Yemeni houses glowing with the sensual hues of burnished copper.

Pauline wanted to know what I thought of the reading, but I suddenly felt like crying and didn't want her to be around.

"Can I please have a moment to collect my thoughts—alone?"

After a long hesitation, my friend assented and left me by the Wallace fountain outside the gate of the tiny public garden—right where we had gotten off the bus, laughing, just a couple of hours ago. Now that garden might have been a postcard picture from a foreign country: I had no sense of where I was. I wanted to sit down—that much I knew. So I did just that, pushing the diminutive picket gate and sitting on one of the benches. The benches were empty, the garden was empty. I had the place to myself.

I was too confused and too worn out to understand what was happening inside me. Still, sitting on that bench, in that silent garden of Montmartre, I gradually came to realize the dawning of something altogether new, in my consciousness and in my vision itself: The marbly pea gravel of the garden path at my feet; the lichen-mottled edging stones of the lawn before me; the dark, gaping cracks between the slabs; the minuscule, spiky tufts of grass, shooting up, star-shaped above the rim of the edging like phosphorescent sparks frozen in midair. It was all so intense and yet so majestically slow, as if a secret world of deep, magical perception was gradually opening up right before my mesmerized eyes.

And the beat of the blood throbbing in my temples—pounding and swishing like the distant din of rollers breaking on sand. That was when I began to hear myself saying the words, over and over, like a talismanic formula: "I'm brave and strong and I can cope."

And how strange it was, all of a sudden: the voice coming out of me, that once trusty vehicle of my will. As strange as the overmagnified creases and crannies of this magically altered garden—deep, shadowy, cracked—and the dreadful lag between the movement of my lips and the sound filling the silence, like an echo returning from a cavernous place somewhere behind me.

A Bridge Too Near:
détournement and the promise of a transnational consciousness

The banner is unambiguous in its edict-like peremptoriness: "No human being is an alien on this earth" (Fig. 1). Attached to the highly estheticized, highly theatricalized Le Pont des Arts—a bridge where amorous promises are exchanged between sweethearts and sealed with an inscribed "love lock"—it is nothing less than a solemn declaration made in the heart of cosmopolitan Paris. Recent memory of a ban on the locks seems only to emphasize the sign's urgency. (The practice of attaching "love locks" to the structure of the bridge was abolished by mayoral decree in 2015. All the padlocks that had accumulated over the years were subsequently removed.) The banner's proclamation (Fig. 2) is an assertive speech act that both appropriates and redefines the performative aspect of the modern-day votive inscriptions formerly affixed to the bridge—the now-prohibited lovers' padlocks (J. L. Austin, *How to Do Things with Words*). Seen in relation to common perceptions of Le Pont des Arts as a univocal symbol of love expressed in terms of a spectacle that is an "expropriation of the Common" (Giorgio Agamben, *The Coming Community*), the banner represents an instance of Situationist *détournement* operating on two interrelated levels (Guy Debord, "Definitions"): on one level, it indexes a neutralization of the bridge's esthetic "aura" (Raoul Vaneigem, "Basic Banalities Part 1"); and on another it marks a strategic "'chiseling'" of the structure's emblematic content—a paring down of its symbolic status as a theatrical site where couples pledge their love to each other in words and through the bond of the padlock (Anselm Jappe, *Guy Debord*). An important characteristic of the banner's *détournement* process thus revolves around its capacity to nullify all potential intertextual references to the bridge's common esthetic-semiological function, "remixing" and redefining the latter by means of a new signifying strategy (Nadine Wanono, "*Détournement* as a Premise"): the "anti-esthetic," disruptive "construction of a milieu" representing "the opposite of quotation" (Debord, "Definitions"; *The Society of the Spectacle*). While constructing a non-common milieu through remixing and redefinition, the banner also manages to generate an alternative semiological context that extends beyond the usual "anti-monumental" effects sought by occupation and *détournement* (Mario Perniola, *Art and its Shadow*). Indeed, what is also at stake here is a simultaneous process of appropriation and supersession of the bridge's shared promissory significance—a shift from the "desiring-

Fig. 1. Le Pont des Arts, Paris, 2018. "No human being is an alien on this earth." Photograph taken by the author.

utterance" of a private declaration promising to bind two people to that of a collective declaration vowing to bind all human beings through the concept of an all-uniting "earth" (Leonard C. Hawes, "Post-Genocide Dialogue").

In this context, one cannot help but recall Michael Ondaatje's "desired" new world and its borderless "cartography" through which people "become nationless" persons "walk[ing] upon [...] an earth that [has] no maps" (*The English Patient*). Announcing the birth of a world in which alienness is abrogated, the sign on the bridge seems to express similar aspirations: first, by redefining its appropriated site in terms of a new *spatial* index—the signifier of a nationless cartography; and second, by articulating it in relation to a new *temporality*—one that supersedes the passé romantic esthetic of the lovers' bridge, presenting a link between the here and now of a nation-centric

Fig. 2. "Love locks" and the declaration of the promise of an unbreakable bond. Photograph taken by the author.

world and the "not-yet" of a "global community" in which everyone becomes a citizen of one nation, the "earth" (Ernst Bloch, *Philosophische Aufsätze*; *Das Prinzip Hoffnung*; Andrew Mason, *Community, Solidarity, and Belonging*). The banner's gesture toward an abrogation of the citizen vs.

alien dichotomy thus places "the pure human" in a new temporal context of radical futurity (Agamben, "Beyond Human Rights"): "*eventum tantum*" as "still-future"—an "infinitive" and "impersonal" moment (Gilles Deleuze, *The Logic of Sense*) announcing nothing less than an imminent recasting of the "Rights of Man" in the form of earth citizenship (Hannah Arendt, *The Origins of Totalitarianism*). The end of alienage as civil and existential condition heralds the coming of a new consciousness "that binds all of humanity to the world's globe" (Michel Serres, *Le Contrat naturel*).

Notwithstanding its anti-esthetic implications, therefore, the banner's proclamation of a transnational consciousness, along with its strategy of *détournement*, invests Le Pont des Arts with expressive content and a mode of temporality that should be conceived primarily in, well, esthetic terms. Call it residual estheticism: a conceptual (as opposed to representational) "esthetic of the event" focused on eliciting public participation through perceptual confrontation rather than identification (Mario Perniola, *Art and its Shadow*). The subjective experience that results from this esthetic revolves around a radically "chiseled" indexical presentation of a central concept-event: the eruption of the strange(r) as the locus of a semiological pair ("*étranger*"/"*étrange*") marking an "estrangement" process—artistic and existential—at the level of the visual itself (Viktor Shklovsky, "Art as Device"). In other words, the mode of alienation indexically expressed by the sign is based on a "tactics of the encounter" whereby the unfamiliarity of the alien as a comforting conceptual signifier of the out-of-the-way and the safely-far-from-home is embodied in textual form and brought as close *to* home as possible, right in the middle of the city (Anja Kanngieser, *Experimental Politics*). In the final analysis, this signifying dynamic underlying the banner's minimalistic event-and-object-based esthetic model points to a particular process of ontological slippage that nullifies the binary opposition between national identity with its various markers (the common, the familiar, the shared) and an indefinite form of identity associated with a mode of being so alien, so unfamiliar that it is equated with the inassimilability of the "stranger" and the "unfamiliar" ("*étranger*").

Considered in relation to the spatiotemporal vision indexed by the sign (the projection of a nationless cartography and a global community to come), the banner's declarative voiding of the national vs. alien binaries confronts us with aspects of "de-severance [*Ent-fernung*]" that make it possible to bridge the "remoteness" of the world the banner is implicitly indicating for us, ushering us into (Heidegger, *Being and Time*). Hence the paradox of this sign as alienating event: its capacity to suddenly bring the "remoteness" ("*Entfernung*") of the strange, the stranger, the alien, and the unfamiliar so close to home even while annulling the (banally homey) closeness of the bridge as a taken-for-granted emblem of the esthetic of love and spectacularized romance. "That which is presumably 'closest' is by no means that which is at the smallest distance 'from us,'" and vice versa (Heidegger, *Being and Time*). The declaration has thus abrogated the status of Le Pont des Arts as a common emblem of national heritage, canceling the spatiotemporal distance the bridge has always sought to keep between the cozy commonness of the local and the always already denied presence of the alien with all the undecidable futurity it incarnates in a world increasingly swept by "vast nomadic" movements of hopeful migrants, a world in which the "strategic political stage [has become] global" and no longer local *thanks* to the nomadic energies of those migrants (Badiou "L'Allégeance à Macron est largement négative!"). Interpreted as a Situationist statement that seeks to deconstruct the familiar esthetic of romance associated with the bridge-as-spectacular-site, the banner forces us to adopt a stance of "concernful circumspection" (Heidegger, *Being and Time*) through its "hijacking" ("*détournement*") of the common signification of the bridge. Beyond its (anti-)esthetic posture, this hijacking compels us to deal with three questions raised by the transgressive placard.

First, there is the question of the banner's enunciatory function in relation to the shared promissory status of the bridge—the amorous declarations and the promise of enduring love that the locks signify. The defamiliarizing eruption of a differently oriented declaration with its own binding ethic—a commitment to an indefinite form of "love," the all-inclusive bond of a transnational consciousness—jarringly, subversively reconstructs a space originally appropriated for the enactment of a binding ritual within the radically *exclusive* sphere of two people. Indeed, the replacement of the metaphoric locks by a sign attached in the same way and to the selfsame structure where the devices once stood is ultimately more than a signifying slippage. It is a deliberate act of superimposition and substitution that is meant to literally foreground an altogether new bond of radical inclusiveness: the token of a world freed from every form of alienness ("*étrangèreté*"), every form of strangeness ("*étrangeté*"), and every form of alienation. The simultaneous appropriation and redefinition of the promissory identity of the bridge in itself thus defines the transgressive presence of the sign as "that something outside and unforeseen [...] something that startles [us] and stares at [us] with alien eyes"; something, in short, that "disturbs the network of the references" and "the fragile sense of *place*, or indeed of *Being itself*" (Gordon, "Displaced"). This transformative power of the sign as that "disturbing [alien] something" not only underlines the votive ardor of *its* promise, it also reveals its confrontational and transgressive intention—its pressing urge to betoken an "ethic of shame" (Zlatan Filipovic), to present itself as a flat statement intended to shame the collective consciousness into envisioning the possibility of an all-inclusive world peopled by "nationless" individuals (Ondaatje, *The English Patient*). Through this act of dissent and confrontation (the jarring note that marks a shift from the esthetic of spectacularized love to an ethic of shame), Le Pont des Arts as a collectively legitimated space of hackneyed romantic performativity and amorous concord becomes a site of productive dissonance and dissidence.

The emergence of this other narrative space through the sheer signifying pregnance of the banner's pronouncement leads us to the question of its transformation of Le Pont des Arts into an interstitial line drawn between two spatiotemporal states—the here and now of a city subjected to the geopolitical logic of a nation-centric world and the not-yet of a nationless earth emancipated from that logic. In other words, the sign forces us to contemplate the full implications of the appropriation and deconstruction of Le Pont des Arts: its transformation from a specific urban site into a *general* emblem of the defamiliarizing emergence of an "atopian" place where the elided other resides: an "in-between space" created by the "the absent [subject] of history"—the repressed alien who is finally granted a place on the bridge, proclaiming the emergence of "an elsewhere that is not yet identifiable" in space-time, "indefinitely other [and] unknown" to "'geometric' or 'geographical' space" (Michel de Certeau, *L'Absent de l'histoire*; "Pratiques d'espace"). In its transgressive novelty, then, the banner manages to metamorphose the bridge into a liminal site in the best sense—a Foucauldian "heterotopia" where a parallel, virtual world and its narrative are created in difference and dissent (Michel Foucault, "Of Other Spaces"). With its alternative declaration, its alternative promise, and its alternative love, the placard's other narrative erupts like an "atopic text" (Roland Barthes, *The Pleasure of the Text* 29) within the master-narrative of nationalism and its "*strategic essentialism*" of nation-centered identity (J. Macgregor Wise, *Cultural Globalization*). To use the famous Deleuze-Guattarian metaphoric conception of the minor subject as an "immigrant" who "walk[s] the tightrope," the reconstruction of the bridge into a space in which an implicit wish is expressed for the cessation of the concepts of immigranthood and alienness signals the appearance of an "outsystem" of signification within the dominant semiological system of the lovers' bridge (Gilles Deleuze and Félix Guattari, *Kafka*; *A Thousand Plateaus*). It is precisely through this outsystem that the emergence of a disruptive meaning *within* the dominant system is made possible: the articulation of a declarative statement that appropriates the promissory logic of the lovers' bond even as it diverges from it radically in its all-inclusive enunciatory logic—a declaration that indexes "no site" and no exclusive recipient, since it "function[s] in [a] total atopia" (Barthes, *Le Plaisir du texte*). The sign is in this respect, conceptually speaking, best apprehended as an operator connecting Le Pont des Arts to a radically other spacetime which nullifies the bridge's prior significance, transforming it into the interstitial site of a wishful projection that augurs the emergence of a new world. Envisioned in Deleuze-Guattarian terms, this brave new world that commences to exist by virtue of those peremptory words uttered in the atopia of Le Pont des Arts is the promise of a bridgehead to the all-inclusive, "transversal" space of a "world-people," a "people to come"—the people of earth citizenship (Gilles Deleuze and Félix Guattari, *What is Philosophy?*).

The banner's announcement of a nationless earth as a transversal space for a world-people to come brings us to the third and last question: the sign's implicit inclusion of the element of ethnic and cultural diversity through the introduction of the alien. Indeed, the placard's appearance on the bridge conjures up a reality that has so far been elided: the common foregrounding of the structure's public function as the "Lovers' Bridge" to the detriment of the staggering ethnic and cultural plurality of the visitors who choose it as the climax of their peregrinations through a city of great ethnic and cultural diversity. In this respect, the presence of the banner on the bridge is quite literally a "*détournement*" (diversion) of the structure's signification through a revelation of the creative hybridity that it embodies day in day out: all those people of different origins converging on the bridge and using it in perfect harmony. "In itself," therefore, Le Pont des Arts is the most eloquent material illustration of Paris's ethnic and cultural diversity—and yet that is not at all the primary characteristic the public think of when they are asked about the symbolic meaning of the bridge. Even so, it is precisely this diverted question that is at the heart of one of the most pressing problems confronting Europe today: the vital roles of ethnic identity and ethnically diverse immigration flows in shaping the socioeconomic and geopolitical future of the "Old Continent." Thus, through its textual conjuring of the in-between, hauntological presence of the alien other, the sign manages to create a powerful linkage between the newly constructed atopian function of the bridge and the alien's unsung existence "living in the interstice"—the rarely estheticized (much less romanticized) "liminality of migrant experience" and its connection to the fact of "hybridity as a contesting, antagonistic [...] political agency" (Homi Bhabha, *The Location of Culture*). In recalling us to the ethnic and cultural diversity of the countless aliens who converge on the bridge, the banner stages yet another message of defamiliarizing confrontation: it urges us to contemplate—by awakening us to the fact that the bridge is one of the most diverse places in Paris—the possibility of a virtual world that is spontaneously transnational and multiethnic; a world, in sum, that succeeds in surpassing the limitations of nation-centrism.

This correlation between transnationalism and the vision of a world of multiethnic coexistence brings me back, in conclusion, to the banner's minimalism in form and expression—the "innocence" and apparent simplicity with which it confronts the public. As mentioned above, the sign's declaration and its promissory drive evoke Ondaatje's vision of a transnational earth, a vision aptly captured by the late Anthony Minghella, whose film adaptation of Ondaatje's novel ends with another declaration: an appeal by Katharine Clifton that can only be interpreted as yet another augury of innocence—a call to bridge the void between the nation-centric here and now and the not-yet of a transnational humanity:

> We die, we die rich with lovers and tribes, tastes we have swallowed [...] I want all this marked on my body. We are the real countries, not the boundaries drawn on maps with the names of powerful men [...] That's all I've wanted—to walk in such a place [...] with friends, an earth without maps. (Anthony Minghella, *The English Patient*)

As envisioned by Minghella, Katharine Clifton's dream of "walk[ing] an earth without maps" embodies a promise that encompasses a unified transnational space (an earth accessible to all), but it is also pertinently accompanied by the communal "we" that marks the unity of all beings, who are now identified no longer as subjects of the "powerful men" but as fluid "tribes" of individuals who, in the corporeality of their natural "bodies," become homologous with the vision of an earth united in a transnational bond—the promise of a "pure human" at last inclusive and compassionate.

The Voice of Exile

In his review of *The Offering*, Wade A Bell Jr makes a cogent analysis of the profound sense of loss and alienation that pervades Tariq Abbassi's tragic life in France, arguing that the radical negativity characteristic of the poet's encounter with European culture revolves around the key question of his existence as a "diasporic body-subject" from North Africa (Wade A Bell Jr, "Salah El Moncef: *The Offering*"). A displaced Tunisian national and trauma victim, Tariq can be seen as an intensified embodiment of the manifold symptoms of shock and dislocation experienced by the Maghrebi diaspora—a poet who adopts the opaque voice of an out-of-place immigrant, with his narrative status eventually becoming a function of the distortions and disjunctions of his mental and corporeal state. While those distortions and disjunctions confront the reader with the daunting challenge of a contradictory consciousness torn between the quest for truth and a radical denial of reality, this selfsame disconnect in Tariq's motives—the unsettling in-between of his double bind—manifests itself in his "fractured" narrative as a potential source of insight for the other (ibid.). When he decides to speak from his space of radical exile (a locus at once of emotional loss and imaginary compensation), Tariq's attempts at a narrative reconstruction of his tragedy turn out to be an ultimate gift to his fellow humans as well as a consuming sacrifice. Faced with the realization that he is out of place both in his native country and in

France—marginalized, stigmatized in both societies—he finds himself embarked on one last desperate endeavor to communicate through the written word.

In this brief response to Bell's commentary on the main character of *The Offering*, I would like to start by considering the unusual terms on which Tariq chooses to make this final gesture at communication, namely, his adamant adherence to a self-narrative that defies causality, logic, and even perceptual sense itself. In the poet's account of an existence burdened with unnamable loss, shorn of any notion of home, the untrammeled imagination remains his only consolation—an inner source of energy that sustains his mental life, the latter being the only realm he can claim as his own after having been stripped of most of his social attributes. The reduction of Tariq's being to pure textuality results in the imagination superseding the dichotomy of truth and falsehood as self-narration becomes his main source of inner meaning and intellectual subsistence. In short, with the factual events of his trauma lost in a zone of radical indeterminacy, the implicit narrative terms dictated by Tariq to the reader are a function of the re-articulation of his life into an account that has moved beyond the confines of ordinary communication to become the expressive vehicle of a shattered sensibility giving voice to its pain within a deeply disjunctive novelistic framework: a narrative continuum of pure intensities (emotional, existential, psychological, sensory-perceptual) rather than a linearly structured text governed by conventional aspects of form, of causal and logical cohesiveness. The voice of a symptom erupting in its raw, radical immediacy. (When viewed within the specific context of Tariq's existential condition, this symptomatic narrative space occupied by the poet seems to be an eerie corollary of his earlier experiences: a singular expressive mode in which the alogical intensity of the exile's voice is proportionate to the extent and severity of his accumulated injuries—the ruthless, ravaging anarchy with which the marks of cultural trauma have come to be inscribed upon the totality of his self, body and mind.) In sum, the elements of intense emotional expression at work in Tariq's self-narration indicate a hypersensitive man confronted with loss and isolation so ineffable that he ends up articulating the extremity of his grief through forms of emotional exteriorization that transcend the conventional logic of narrative expression—affective singularities that cannot be grasped in terms of such conceptual binaries as truth/falsehood, logic/illogic, reason/unreason. In other words, Tariq's last gesture of communication with his fellow humans is a mode of expression that is as aporetic as his in-between position; an act best understood as the narrative equivalent of a primal scream: the expression—radical, raw, unmediated by logic or causality—of a sense of malaise so deep that it cannot be brought into coherent expression. Paradoxically, it is within this narrative space of profound loss, of grief and powerlessness beyond articulation, that Tariq finds his most eloquent voice as a writer.

Let us recall here that the artist's ultimate exile—his confinement within a heterogeneous text articulated as a field of affective singularities—represents the culminating point of a life marked by real and symbolic exile since his college days in Tunisia. The "road to Brittany" and the trauma center is in this respect the culminating point in a life characterized by a profound sense of homelessness that makes him feel out of place both in his native country and in France—doomed to be marginalized and stigmatized in both societies (Salah el Moncef, *The Offering*). Faced with these negative aspects of social in-betweenness, Tariq embraces rather than resists his condition—affirming his marginal existence within the artist's inner universe, opting for the imaginary compensation the latter presents. As Bell aptly puts it, even while this radical choice puts the poet in a position of intense solitude, there is a persistent, haunting quality of universality in Tariq's stand, one that suffuses his story with a certain existential genericity, making us apprehend his personal shock as far more than the ethnicity specific experience of a North African man confronted with the challenges of stigmatization and exclusion. This particular characteristic of Tariq's existential state—an element pertaining to readerly identification—requires further elaboration, for it points to aspects of transnational selfhood that extend beyond the specificities of his condition and their expression in narrative form.

⁂

Noting certain features of universality in Tariq's narrative, Bell argues that *The Offering* "contains ... elements that are relatable to ... the experiences of others who might share more similar experiences" with him ("Salah El Moncef: *The Offering*"). The story's potential for creating feelings of identification among diasporic readers of various identities brings us to another of Tariq's paradoxes: the fact that the symptoms of disjunction and homelessness that have contributed to the disintegration of the man's life are inextricably connected with the principles of tolerance, openness and global identification that have made him, from the beginning of his intellectual and artistic career, the quintessential transnational subject—a "world citizen" endowed with a natural capacity to interface between different modes of belief, different cultural heritages and practices. Notwithstanding Tariq's deeply flawed character, his unusually adaptable identity is ultimately an admirable component of his personality, for it allows him to accept and live by a rather arduous life principle: his firm belief that the transnational life is the only life he wants to live, in spite of the ravages of racist hatred and violence. During his residence in Bordeaux, he faces those ravages with fortitude and chooses to project the universalistic ideal of a fundamental affinity between human beings—a positive urge that makes them seek to develop meaningful ties with one another in spite (or perhaps *because*) of their differences. A genuine Anzaldúan "crosser of cultures," Tariq finds certitude in the ethos of the transnational self that he is, asserting the creative power of difference in the face of intolerance and conformity (Gloria Anzaldúa, *Borderlands/La Frontera*). More than a geopolitical reality, the transnational experience that he lives is deeply rooted in his consciousness—a form of second nature stemming from the realization early on in his life that the fact of hybridity and in-betweenness is not a source of existential anxiety but an integral part of his quest to realize his full potential as a thinker and as an artist. Through his cosmopolitan intellectual and artistic choices in Tunisia and in France, Tariq has come implicitly to endorse cultural and social energies that subvert real and symbolic borders—geopolitical, ethnic, religious, linguistic, and cultural. The trinational family he creates in France with his German wife is proof that he espouses progressive dynamics of hybridity and transnational identifications—existential choices that imply radical transformations, which he undertakes with admirable tolerance of mind and flexibility of character. For a brief period of time in his life, the voice of exile that characterizes his poetic sensibility seems to be, despite the many challenges, an invigorating sign of plurality and innovation rather than a symptom of alienation. While there is an urge in his writings to historicize and narrativize his self as an ethnically and culturally specific form of *being* who exists in a European country, there is a much stronger tendency both in his work and in his sensibility to envision his self as the sum of a *becoming*—a process of transformation, through his relationships and his creative work, into a "plastic man," a synthesizing subject "permeable to [new] principles" and rejoicing in a conception of his existence as the locus of shifting identifications, a space of displacement in a transformative sense (Ralph Waldo Emerson, "Self-Reliance"). In sum, although Tariq rarely reflects consciously on his plural identity and identifications, it is important to note the extraordinary ethical dimension of this achievement from a man whose consciousness ends up evolving over the years into a site of cultural multiplicity. As a tangible indicator of this multiplicity, the dynamics of hybridity and transnational identification at work in the family founded by Tariq and his wife point to the question of immigration in Europe as a potential force of social renewal through diversity: the novel forms and spaces of identity formation that immigration creates within the monolithic logic of the nation-state, deconstructing its reductive myths of nationhood, territory, citizenship, and Eurocentric ethnic identity.

Thus, in spite of the monolithic cultural environment in which he finds himself after Paris, Tariq's unspoken vision of his identity as a transnational artist and as a plastic man who wants to contribute to a new Europe represents both a hopeful force of change and a factor of immense challenge for the artist who has decided to leave the capital in order to make a living and fulfill his literary aspirations in *La Province*. Indeed, what he finds in Bordeaux is the radical opposite of his ideal vision of Europe as an integrative space based on a synthesization of the energies of diverse cultural and ethnic forces. Provincial France turns out to be a space in which the exclusion and stereotyping of Arabs and North Africans is common practice. In spite of the deep existential shock created by the stigmatizing forces that he is confronted with after his separation from his wife and children, Tariq opts not to seek moral support in the Maghrebi community. Rather, he chooses to further affirm the interstitial character of his subject position and life choices. And while this momentous existential decision ends up radicalizing the poet's solitary, individualistic existence in Bordeaux, it also makes his account of his provincial experience suffused by an implicit awareness of his connection to diasporic subjects like him, men and women from different backgrounds who conceive of our postmodern world as a borderless space. It is primarily in relation to his commitment to this borderless world vision that we should envision Tariq's avoidance of a "return" to the North African community; a deeply ethical commitment indeed that helps him maintain the transnational character of his life as well as his art, with both remaining the space of an interstitial articulation between North and South. Considered in the context of Tariq's self-narrative, the double articulation of his identity in terms of European and North African belonging can be seen as the site of an intersection through which the pluralistic vision of the plastic man becomes increasingly linked to his mode of narration. As the account of his interstitial existence between the North and the South, Tariq's story is in this respect an innovative esthetic force that allows him to creatively appropriate different markers of social and cultural commonality: symbols of national identity that he transforms into the subjective referents of a consciousness dwelling between nations and their common social and cultural identifications.

The vision of narrative space as the scene of a transnational self consciously (ethically) cultivating an artistic sensibility of the in-between refers us to a defining characteristic of Tariq's conception and expression of the time-place-affect nexus: his imaginary appropriation and reconstruction of the settings that he revisits neither in European terms nor in North African terms, but in terms of the voice of the exile—a voice through which socially and culturally overdetermined spaces are apprehended as fluid, shifting sites of existential and affective self-projection rather than as sites of national or even cultural identification/identity. The poet's deeply personal, idiosyncratic way of relating to space through narrative results in a singular conception of temporality, one that is marked by a permanent quality of disjunction whose main characteristic in Tariq's account is the incessant, dizzying interplay of radically different spatiotemporal experiences: impressions juxtaposed into a fluid collage of referents from European and Mediterranean history and heritage—socially and culturally overdetermined indexes of national identity embedded into Tariq's multimedia text as a deeply personal assemblage of topographical, archeological, esthetic, and architectural references. In the final analysis, as the effect of a fluid collage, the meanings and representations that emerge from Tariq's disjunctive text index a sense of spatiotemporality that is determined by his multi-experiential consciousness—a synthetic, plural, and postnational consciousness by definition.

※

These elements of spatiotemporality in Tariq's narrative—and the particular dynamics of appropriation and transformation they imply—bring us to another paradoxical aspect of the artist's persona: the articulation of his subjectivity in terms of a dialectic of difference that makes it possible for the reader to apprehend his experience as a "third element" born of the North-South encounter and signifying the traumas as well as the potentials of colonial and postcolonial history (Anzaldúa, *Borderlands/La Frontera*). Indeed, while the poet's in-between subject position in France is an index of alienation and marginalization, that selfsame position represents a potential site of intellectual and artistic enrichment thanks to his "different status" as a diasporic subject. It is precisely through Tariq's traumatic experience of stigmatization, marginalization, and alienation that the reader manages to see in his account of life between Europe and North Africa a narrative of great critical promise: a testimony that gestures toward the possibility of reconceptualizing European society into a space operating on the basis of inclusion and synthesization of divergent cultural forces rather than on the basis of the "management" of those forces as "ethnic minorities" in need of "integration." Ultimately, the story's dramatization of Tariq's in-betweenness as a form of interstitiality that is as radical as it is irresolvable—the articulation of his existence *between* North African and European identities, the marginality of his voice *within* both—refers us to the twin questions of national belonging and citizenly "allegiance," a central problematic in the life of a man whose identity cannot be defined in terms of conventional citizenship. As the locus of transnational sensibilities and identifications that surpass the boundaries of the nation-state, Tariq's subject position obliges us to reflect on the presence of the immigrant other beyond the local/national terms of belonging and citizenship (either Tunisian or French) and in the global terms of transnational selfhood (*both* Tunisian and French).

It is in this specific context that Tariq's narrative reveals one of its most significant characteristics as the testimonial text of a diasporic subject-body, indicating its pertinence to the current globalization-migration debate and, by the same token, its function as a potential site of identification and reflection for various diasporic subjects, especially those who are working toward a redefinition of their relation to their cultural heritage outside the reductive framework of national belonging. While this redefinition process is still in its infancy in many countries, the time has never been more propitious for the diasporic subject to negotiate and rethink her identity in terms of an interfacing between various identity categories and a potential synthesization of those categories into a novel form of self— an interstitial, "transcategorial self" (Moncef, "Übermenschen, Mestizas, Nomads"). In short, a new form of plastic womanhood or manhood that refuses rigid adherence to reductive forms of self-definition, finding new existential meaning in the affirmation of interstitiality in all its forms: transnational, transcultural, transidiomatic, transtextual—in short, *transformational*. Ultimately, concretizing this new transformational horizon of the plastic individual—the future subject of the transnational public sphere—remains one of the most urgent questions of our time, pressing us to rethink the irreversible globalization of our world, to reconceptualize its immense possibilities for cultural enrichment and peaceful coexistence as well as its dire potential for culture shock and conflict.

CPSIA information can be obtained
at www.ICGtesting.com
Printed in the USA
LVHW100702171022
730846LV00007B/120/J